LEVEL PLAYING FIELDS
John Costello

Jaycee Books

Table of Contents

To all my family and friends.

Chapter 1 On The Run

Joey climbed through the fence, picked up the bag he'd thrown over it, struck out across the field. It was a pleasant day with the sun up and warming nicely. The time was ten-thirty a.m. The grass beneath his feet was wet with the heavy overnight dew and clung to his shoes and trouser legs as he hurried along.

So far, so good. No one had seen him. All he had to do now was cross the field into the lane, walk fifty yards to the railway station and catch a train to London. Then he would be safe.

He had made up his mind that morning to go absent. He, Joey Webster, a corporal in the Royal Air Force with only a month's service left to complete, was going absent without official leave. He'd been put on a charge and frog marched up in front of the commanding officer.

"I will not tolerate such behaviour, Corporal," Group Captain Small said to him earlier, his fat gin-gut flopping over the edge of his desk. His out of condition appearance was undoubtedly the result of his excessive drinking over the years in the Officer's Mess bar that Joey was only too aware of. "And especially not from you, Webster, with your position of trust and responsibility, that is. Despicable! What on earth got into you, my boy?"

He stood there with sergeant Cummins breathing down the back of his neck. "I. . .I don't know, sir."

"Have you anything to say for yourself, Corporal?"

What could he say? What did the fat-gutted bastard expect him to say? His words and two stripes didn't count for much against hot-lipped Lawrence's commission and posh bloody accent; he knew that, the lying bitch!

"Only that I'm sorry for what I have done, sir," he said finally.

"I should bloody well think so, too. Do you realize I could have you put inside for what you did?"

"Yes, sir."

1

"Drunk, whilst in charge of the Officer's Mess! Assaulting a WAF officer! Striking Sergeant Cummins! What on earth were you playing at, boy?"

"But, sir, she-"

"-She, Webster?"

"Officer Lawrence, sir. She-"

"-Quiet, boy!"

Then Silence.

"These are damned serious charges, Corporal."

Then a rustling of papers on Small's desk in front of him.

"I see you have only a month's service to complete before demobilization, Webster?"

"Yes, that is correct, sir."

Silence.

Then: "I'm going to be lenient with you, Corporal. Seeing as you have so little time left to serve, and taking into account your past good record . . . However, you will still have to pay the penalty for your disgraceful behaviour. Therefore I am going to reduce you to the ranks and confine you to your barracks for fourteen days. And you can count yourself lucky, my boy! Case dismissed!"

Sergeant Cummins then escorted him back to his billet and left him sitting on the edge of his bed while he went to attend duties back at the mess. Good riddance to him and all, he thought. If it hadn't been for him then Joey might never have found himself in this present predicament.

He had been lucky, he knew that. The C.O. could have put him inside, but hadn't. Not that any of it had been entirely his fault anyway. Flight Officer Lawrence was the real cause of all the bother after a party in the mess. He had just finished clearing up for the night when there was a tap on the door. He unlocked it to find her standing there in the darkened corridor.

"Could I possibly trouble you for some cigarettes, Corporal?" she asked quietly.

"Certainly, Ma'am," he answered politely, going behind the bar to get them. When he turned, he found her perched on the barstool. The door was shut tight.

"You're very kind." She smiled, and then whispered: "Any chance of a gin and tonic before turning in? I'm terribly thirsty."

It's more than a gin and tonic she's after, Corporal Webster, Joey thought to himself. Look at her - she's half pissed!

"Just a wee one, Corporal?"

He hesitated, sensing danger. She offered him a cigarette, which he accepted along with a light from her lighter that she brought in to action out of her small bag on top of the bar as she looked across at him with drowsy blue eyes.

"How about that drink?"

"God almighty! She's had more than enough," he said to himself. "Look at her eyes - she can't even talk properly."

"No one need know. Just the two of us, eh? Everyone else has turned in for the night. It's much too hot for that, don't you think? Let's have some iced drinks to cool ourselves down with, shall we? You will join me, won't you, Corporal?"

He plumped for scotch, knowing that he shouldn't really; but his weaker side got the better of him and he succumbed to temptation.

"Make them doubles. God! It's hot."

He prepared their drinks. When he turned, she'd slipped off her tunic and tie.

"There, that's more comfortable," she said, smiling at him.

He gulped his drink.

"A busy evening, Corporal?"

"Yes, Ma'am, very."

"Just one thing wrong with it, I found. I didn't see what I would call a real man anywhere." She swallowed a good measure of her drink. "You do know what I mean, Corporal?"

He felt himself being drawn into something he shouldn't. Rather like an unsuspecting butterfly about to be caught in a net.

"Not really, no, Ma'am," he tried dismissing the officer's remark without offending her.

"Of course you do, silly."

He felt pressured. "Yes, Ma'am, if you say so."

"And you can drop that Ma'am talk, Corporal."

Silence followed.

Then: "Please don't pay any attention to me, I've had a bad mood all evening." She finished her drink. "Let's have another for the road, shall we? What is your name, by the way?"

He finished his drink also. "Webster, Ma'am. Corporal Joey Webster."

"Hello, Joey - I'm Doreen."

He replenished their empty glasses.

"How long have you been running the bar then, Joey?"

"'Bout three and a half years, Ma'am."

"Do call me Doreen. . ."

"Doreen . . . Ma'am."

They drank and talked for what must have been a good hour. By now he was feeling the effects of their continual drinking. Officer Lawrence, he noticed, looked well and truly under its influence. It was then that it happened. In trying to light a cigarette, the officer managed to drop her lighter on the floor. "Oh, hell!" she murmured angrily. With difficulty she then asked: "C-could you poshh...ibly retrieve it for me, Joey?"

He obliged, and then offered to light her cigarette. But she suddenly slid down from her stool and slipped her arms around his neck. He felt her well-shaped body close to his, exciting him. Then their lips met and they were both kissing each other passionately. The bar door then opened.

"How dare you?" the officer suddenly screamed, slapping him hard across the face. "S-Sergeant! This man's just assaulted me."

He swung round, his face stinging from her blow to find the large physique of sergeant Cummins framed in the open doorway.

"Is this correct, Corporal?" Cummins demanded an explanation.

"N-no, Sarge," he stammered, holding his cheek and in a complete state of shock at the officer's sudden change of behaviour towards him.

"I'm telling you he. . .he's just molested me!" officer Lawrence screamed at the sergeant hysterically.

"Do you wish to press charges, Ma'am?" Cummins sounded unsure of himself, having never been confronted with a situation such as this before. Judging by the look on his face though, he was thoroughly enjoying his moment of glory.

"Yes, Sergeant I most certainly do," her tone of voice being most emphatic.

"But, Sarge, she-"

"-Hold your tongue! Webster. . . Now, Ma'am - just what happened here?"

Officer Lawrence then went on to explain to Cummins her reason for being in the bar. She then went on to say that the corporal had offered her a drink. She knew she was breaking mess rules concerning after time drinking, but found no serious harm in it seeing as the corporal had still more work to do before closing down for the night. She had found it very warm, hence the removal of her tunic. All this she spoke in a very sober manner indeed, considering the amount of drink she'd consumed. "But it gave the Corporal no right doing what he did," she continued, even more soberly. "You saw him fondling me, didn't you, Sergeant?"

"Yes, Ma'am, I most certainly did. You just leave everything to me now - I'll see to it that the Corporal's charged accordingly, Ma'am."

"Thank you so much, Sergeant."

"You run along now, Ma'am."

It would have been no good trying to talk his way out of the predicament he now found himself in. Cummins hated his guts. The feeling was mutual also. They'd never hit it off together, always at each other's throats. He would take immense pleasure seeing Joey in trouble. Not that the man was of unblemished character himself. Joey knew a thing or two about his dealings with the catering officer and the fiddle going on between them and the station's meat wholesalers these last few years, didn't he? He certainly had no room to shout, had he? He could have argued with the man about what had just happened, but what good would it have done? His word against an officer's? He didn't stand a chance. He was outranked on all sides.

Cummins stood there, a smile on his ugly, pockmarked face. "It's the bloody high jump for you, Webster," he sneered.

"You wouldn't be interested to know that it was the lady who made a play for me, would you, Sarge?" Joey attempted an explanation of what actually took place between him and the officer.

"No, Corporal, I wouldn't. Now. . . if you'll lock up, I'll escort you down to my office. And that's an order! Webster."

"You can go to hell!"

"You're in enough trouble already without further adding to it, Webster. Now - for the last time, will you obey my command?"

"Not before doing just one more thing first, Sarge." Something that Joey had looked forward to for a long time.

"And what pray, is that?"

"To give you a bloody good hiding, that's what, pal."

Cummins reacted quickly, raising both hands to shield his face; but he was too late as Joey hit him with a right, square on the jaw. The blow sent him spinning out through the open door where he hit the wall in the corridor and slid down it in a heap on the floor.

"That's for being such a nosey bastard!" Joey growled at him angrily, leaning against the bar to watch Cummins humiliatingly pick himself up from the floor.

"D-do you realize what you've just done, Webster?" he mumbled, a thin trickle of blood appearing at the corner of his swollen mouth.

"Something I should have done ages ago, that's what," Joey confessed to the sergeant, swaying slightly where he stood now upright, wondering whether Cummins would come back in the bar to make a fight of it.

But Cummins just stood there pointing a finger at him, saying: "You'll get busted for this, Webster! Mark my words."

Joey took a step forward. "Go to bloody hell!" he yelled, kicking the bar door shut in his face.

And today when he had gone before the commanding officer to have his stripes taken away, he'd made up his mind to just walk straight out of camp and go AWOL. What had he to lose? If only that sex-starved officer had thrown the lock on the door then none of this nasty business need have happened. She had come looking for trouble, had created it and had got off scot-free. She'd only been stationed on the camp a couple of months. He could remember her coming in the bar her first day in the mess. She was rather forward then, smiling at him, saying she'd see him later that evening for a drink. Quite an attractive woman really, aged late thirties, he guessed. She certainly had a good figure and held herself well. Little did he know she would be the cause of all his bother? Pity, because he quite liked her. But then, one should never trust a woman, so they say. Besides, she was officer material. Not too fussy which officer either. She had them all running around after her. Especially during their monthly dining in nights. Joey could recall disturbing her and whoever was taste of the month on numerous occasions during their lovemaking moments in various dark corners of the mess. It didn't seem to bother her or her companions though.

One night of particular interest to those who witnessed it, occurred quite recently. It started in the bar after the officer's had finished eating their evening meal in the adjoining dining room, with all of them looking prim and proper in their short, bum-freezer dress uniforms, this whole procedure being supervised by Joey's arch- enemy, sergeant Cummins, catering coming under his jurisdiction. Although it was Joey's ultimate responsibility for the distribution of wine during the meal, and, later, for the successful manoeuvring of the port and sherry decanters around the tables for use by the officers in response to the countless number of toasts being offered, the sergeant always made his presence felt as he hovered in the wings waiting to pounce if Joey happened to neglect the replenishment of any of the officers glasses when required. He took great delight in this, for there were occasions when this would happen, despite all available catering personnel being on duty for that night. With the completion of the usual speeches and the raising of glasses and the smoking of cigars reserved for these occasions, the officers then adjourned to the bar to continue further drinking and merriment until the early hours of the morning. The evening had been a fairly quite one compared to most. In the past, Joey had actually seen officers clearing a space in the dining area once these formalities had concluded to participate in a mock- up game of rugby, using the empty punch bowl as a ball which would invariably end up considerably the worse for wear and losing the use for which it was originally intended. With the absence of the rugby match on this night in question, those present no doubt felt the need for some other form of recreation to stimulate them. A car race was suggested by one of the senior officers. This would take place on the road outside that conveniently encircled the mess building and camp sports field. Each car was to have a co-driver of their choice. A youthful looking RAF Regiment officer opened a book to give odds and to take bets on who would win the race. There had been some concern shown over this, as it was a well-known fact that the officer in question had the reputation of being somewhat of a gambler and apparently owed quite a considerable amount of money to a local bookmaker. He was also a bit of a ladies man, and what probably wouldn't be well known was that recently he had secretly taken nude photographs of a WAAF officer he was having a fling with on camp and which Joey had been given the privilege of seeing by courtesy of his batman who had found them lying about in his quarters one day. The snaps proved to be of a very revealing nature indeed. If only the poor lady in question knew of this, she wouldn't be very well pleased, Joey thought. The bookies favourite to win the race of which six drivers and their passenger were competing was the bar officer, squadron leader Weller, Joey's boss who owned an open topped sports car which he enjoyed putting to the test when ever an opportunity arose, especially as there was in this case a chance of winning some prize money. All wagers were placed behind the bar for safe keeping, Joey being given this responsibility.

With all of these formalities completed, there was then a mass exodus from the bar to outside where those involved positioned their vehicles behind a line by the lighted entrance to the mess to await the signal for the start of the race. The winner would be the first car to pass this position after successfully completing six laps of the circular roadway.

The contest was got under way by one of the senior officer's ringing a large bell handed to him by one of his fellow colleagues amidst wild, loud cheering from those gathered to witness this spectacle.

Joey, not being able to leave the bar unattended, had to be content to watch from behind the open mess window along with a few other officers who decided to do likewise by not venturing outside. From this position they could see the actual start to the race as the contestants with their illuminated car headlights to guide their journey in the night darkness, sped past them with a roar of engines and screech of tyres on the gravelled driveway as they disappeared out of sight behind the mess in a trail of smoke.

Approximately two minutes later they were to return with beeping horns and a crunching of gears but with the vehicles more spaced out now as they jostled for positions on completing the first lap, with squadron leader Weller, the favourite, in the lead by just a bonnet's length from his nearest opponent, the co-driver of which was seen leaning out of his open window and shouting at the top of his voice to catch, ". . .that bastard Sam Weller up!"

Ten minutes later, the race was completed, with the bar officer way out in front as the winner. The driver in last position, whose passenger just happened to be the same lady involved with him in the nude picture episode, appeared not to have the slightest interest in winning the rally for they were both busily engaged in a pastime of a far more urgent nature. At least to them it was, anyway, because they could be quite visibly seen going through the motions of making love together as the WAAF officer in the front seat of the car sat astride her driver as they sped past the mess in a climatic finish for the pair of them with their car shuddering to a halt on the grass verge outside the mess. These two received as much, if not more applause from the onlookers for their efforts than did squadron leader Weller for actually winning the race.

"Well done! What!"

"All for Queen and country!"

"Stupendous performance, ol' boy!"

A champagne reception greeted all the competitors in the race back in the bar afterwards which kept Joey busy till the early hours of the morning with those in question getting up to even more larking about before everyone decided to call it a day. Joey couldn't help but wonder how they managed to get away with such behaviour. After all, weren't they supposed to be officers and gentlemen and above such antics? He, on the other hand, and being of lower rank, had stepped out of line just the once and had been for the high jump, hadn't he?

If only that stupid sergeant hadn't come barging in on him and officer Lawrence the way he did that night, then none of these problems needed have arisen. Bloody idiot! He and Joey never did see eye to eye over the years together. Cummins always gave him the impression that he was jealous of his position behind the bar and in the company of officers all the time. He also didn't like Joey playing cricket for the station cricket team either. In fact, Joey was quite a good cricketer, having tried his hand at this profession prior to enlisting in the Air Force. He'd actually spent three seasons engaged on the staff at Lord's Cricket Ground.

After leaving school at the age of fifteen and with no education qualifications whatsoever, he found the only thing that he was exceptionally good at was playing cricket. So he decided to become a professional cricketer. Just like that. He tried hard, but lacked the application needed for this career. So he left Lord's to join the RAF, thinking that this might be a more suitable proposition for him. He signed on for a four-year term with them when he was eighteen, and was promoted to corporal in his third year of service. Lately, however, he found himself becoming restless as his time with them drew to a close. The outside world seemed to beckon his return. No doubt this business with officer Lawrence would ultimately lead him on to pastures new?

"Sod them all!" he said out loud, striding across the field on his way to the railway station. He'd have a fortnight in London away from it all. The warm July weather looked like continuing and it would be nice making the most of it. He wouldn't worry himself about the outcome of his actions. At least when he returned, the gossip concerning him and the officer in question would have died down. After that - demobilization.

He started humming a tune cheerfully to himself, his bag slung over his shoulder, the field sloping away to the left. He came down the slope, happy with the sun on his back, the grass wet beneath his feet, the birds singing, and full of the excitement of the day and what he was about to do. Once in London he would stay at a small hotel somewhere and spend days touring the city. He might even go to Lord's to watch the cricket. The more he thought of it, the better he liked the idea altogether.

No one had seen him sneak out of his billet to come down into the field that ran behind the camp. Now he was on his own. He could see the gate at the bottom of the slope and the hedge running either side of it where the field ended. He was careful to avoid the cowpats scattered about at various intervals. He could see no cattle anywhere though. No doubt they were resting someplace. From over in the lane he heard an electric train moaning as it pulled out of the station.

Won't be long now, he thought, increasing his step. It was then that it happened. From behind, disturbing the pleasant peacefulness he'd been enjoying, came a frightening snorting noise and the sound of something heavy moving toward him.

He swung round, the muscles in his body tense, and his mind alert; but for a brief moment, both mind and body froze simultaneously, unable to think or move. For his eyes, opened wide, saw, charging down on him from the slope above, a black, ferocious looking bull, its ugly twisted horns and thick neck plainly visible standing as he was no more than thirty yards or so away.

"My God!" he exclaimed out loud, his voice sounding strange out in the middle of the field, but bringing him horrifyingly back to life.

With his heart thumping wildly, he turned and ran fast down the remaining slope of the field, the same distance between him, the gate and safety, as between him and the charging bull. For some terrifying moments he thought he wasn't going to make it in time. Then, there it was in front of him, his legs having moved swifter than they'd ever done in their life before, while all the time at the back of him, the bull, crashing through the grass, the sound of it like thunder in his ears, until finally, feeling it so close at his heels he very nearly messed his pants, he took off. In one swift movement he threw his bag out in front of him, dived clear over the top of the gate, landed safely on the other side and rolled down the grassy bank into the lane.

He got to his feet. He was all right. He noticed his bag resting above him on the bank. He could hear his heart beating noisily like a big bass drum inside him as his body heaved up and down vigorously, gasping for breath. He peered through the gate at the bull. The bull stared back at him, snorted, lowered his head and rammed at the gate. Then again, and again, the gate shaking precariously, and Joey frightened to death lest it should force it open.

He looked up and down the lane. No one. What was he to do? He had to rescue his bag - a change of clothing and toothbrush were inside. The gate above him rattled and shook as the bull continued butting. Should he risk it? He took a deep breath, was about to scramble up after his belongings, when, from the corner of his eye, he spotted a pile of rubble dumped beneath an old oak tree a few yards further along the lane to his left.

He hurried down to it, hoping to find something to hurl at the enraged bull. He spotted them immediately at the foot of the pile. House bricks! A score of them at least, along with empty cement bags, broken lavatory pans, sheets of torn wallpaper.

Joey dived in after them, clawing at them eagerly just as if they had been gold nuggets glinting up at him in the sunshine that filtered through the green foliage of the tree above. He picked out four good ones, cradled them in his arms, turned and advanced toward the bull, who, it appeared, had stopped its horn-butting and was now tail-swishing and looking inquisitively over the top of the gate at him.

He halted in the lane by the gate, staring him straight in the eye. The bull lowered its horned head to ram again.

"Ah..!" Joey shouted at the beast. "Ah..!"

The brute raised his head quickly.

"That's it, bull, look me in the eye!" Joey growled at it angrily, stepping bravely up on to the grass bank, clutching tight to his bricks. "You bastard! You bloody bastard! With his breathing improved and through his angriness finding new strength and courage, he gripped one of the bricks securely in the palm of his right hand and raised it high above his head. "This is for you, Sergeant Cummins!" he hissed, taking careful aim.

The bull, pawing the ground, snorted at him aggressively as Joey brought his arm down with as much force as his body could render and let the brick fly. It hit the animal squarely on the tip of its muzzle. The bull snorted again, tossing his large ugly head backwards, blood spurting from its nostrils. Again and again it shook its head, spraying blood everywhere.

"Take that! sodding officer Small!" Joey shouted jubilantly, another brick in his hand ready to hurl at the enraged bull.

The bull took evasive action by moving away from him.

Greedy for revenge, he clambered through the gate in pursuit of it. He let fly another missile, this time hitting officer bloody Lawrence right up the backside! The raging bull turned tail and made off.

"Come back!" he cried, giving chase. He had ammunition left and was eager to use it. "Come back here!"

But the bull had had enough and was gaining ground on him fast. And then there was somebody shouting: "Hey! You! What you think you're playing at?"

He saw a figure of a man standing further up in the field brandishing a stick and waving it at him furiously. "What the hell you up to?"

Joey stopped dead in his tracks. The man was now striding toward him. He dropped his remaining brick supply to the ground, V-signed the intruder on his way to greet him, turned and ran off. The last thing he wanted was a scene with some angry old farmer

He climbed hurriedly back over the gate, picked up his bag and raced off down the lane in the direction of the railway station, not once looking back.

He arrived just as a train pulled in. Purchasing a ticket to Baker Street, he boarded it, the slide doors hissing shut behind him. He sat himself down at the rear of the compartment, panting heavily from his excursions. He looked around. The carriage was empty. Putting his feet up on the seat opposite, he gazed through the window, the green-grassed embankments outside racing past as the train increased speed. Joey smiled to himself, the smile then slowly broke into a chuckle, the chuckle developed into a snigger, until finally, throwing his head back and holding tight to his sides, he burst forth into an uncontrollable fit of laughter, the train rattling along noisily beneath him.

"That bastard bull!" he shouted down the empty compartment between convulsions. "That bloody red-nosed bastard bull!"

The train slid into a tunnel, the wheels pounding out a steady rhythm on the metal tracks that snaked out in front of them towards London.

Chapter 2 London

Joey lay stretched out on his back in Regent's Park dozing. Now, on awakening, but with his eyes still closed, he could hear the familiar sounds he had heard before going to sleep. Small children shrieked and laughed as they played; a gentle breeze rustled the leaves high in the tops of the trees that ran along down behind the iron rail fence at the back of him toward the edge of the lake. He could hear again the oars from the rowing boats out on the lake being worked in their metal sockets and of them dipping in the water, the birds singing, the ducks quaking, and even some bees buzzing off to his left over by the pathway where the colourful flowerbeds were arranged.

He lay listening to these sounds with his eyes shut for quite some time. He felt really happy and excited, because for the next couple of weeks he would do the things he wanted. He felt free - was his own master, without having to bother about kowtowing to those stuff shirt officers in the mess every day. In his opinion they were all a bunch of bloody morons anyway, each trying to outrank the other as they tried justifying their positions of self-importance. He doubted very much that any of them could ever make a go of it back outside in civvy street, convinced they would all be like fish out of water really, left floundering without the necessary knowledge of how to survive in this completely different environment to the one they were accustomed to. He almost felt sorry for them in an odd sort of way, despite their advantages in life.

He wondered if they had missed him back at camp yet, and guessed that they must have. Sergeant Cummins would question his absence, that's for sure. And the bar officer would certainly be in a right flap over it. Joey wouldn't worry about it though. He'd made up his mind to go through with this and wanted to forget all about the Air Force for the time being. He would have a relaxing fortnight on his own. What with the commanding officer's business earlier and the episode with that crazed bull, it certainly had been an eventful day so far. If that was anything to go by, he could well be in for an exciting time.

He had come straight up to Regent's Park after arriving safely at Baker Street and leaving his bag at the left luggage office. He knew of a small hotel in Gloucester Place that would suit him admirably for his stay in London and would check in there later. For the time being he would relax in the sun and give some thought to his plan of action. To start with, he would need some new clothes. Then, after fixing himself up with accommodation, he would check to see if there was any cricket being played at Lord's and maybe go along there later after having a meal somewhere.

Joey could feel the grass beneath him damp with the warmth from his body. He felt the grass with the palms of his outstretched hands beside him. He had always liked the feel and smell of grass, especially new-mown. He probably associated it with the game of cricket and was reminded of the lush, green sports grounds he had played on in the past.

He felt in his back pocket to check that his money was safe. Yes, the roll of notes with an elastic band round them was still there. A wallet would have been safer really. He didn't like them though. Jock Wilson, a waiter back at the mess used a purse to keep his money in, he remembered. Joey didn't like Jock Wilson. He didn't like anyone who hated parting with their money the way he did from his silly little purse. He remembered going out drinking with the lads many times in the past and of how difficult it always was in getting that old skinflint to stand a round.

Slowly Joey opened his eyes, and then shut them again quickly. It was too bright everywhere and the sunlight hurt them. He raised his arm, resting it on his forehead as a shield, and then opened them again cautiously. Squinting at first, but then gradually becoming accustomed to the light, he looked out from beneath his arm. The sky above appeared to be off-white in colour; but after blinking a few times and opening his eyes wide, he then saw that the vast expanse was as blue and clear as he had ever seen it before.

"God!" he uttered to himself in amazement. "What a beautiful sky!"

He lay looking up, marvelling at the greatness of it all. It sure was a blue sky all right. It just went on and on, and up and up and up. And from way up there in the blue he spotted a plane. It made no noise as it moved slowly across the sky, showing silver in the sunlight like a solitary fish roaming the spacious seas.

"You're alone, plane," he addressed the distant object in space. "Like me, you are all alone. You're right up there and I'm way down here, and we're both all alone."

The plane suddenly disappeared from sight.

We're not alone really though, Joey thought, still gazing up at the sky, the sun, to his right, blazing down. The plane has people on board, and there are also people down here with me. If anyone's alone it's the sky. Her nearest friends are the stars and the moon and the sun. And just think how far away they all are?

Joey sat up, rubbed his eyes. Eventually, the scene focused more clearly for him as he observed the numerous boats out on the lake, the water glistening bright in the sunlight and the wooden seats beneath the trees on the other side of the lake with people sitting there and ducks waddling to and fro in front of them. He noticed the heavy iron bridge spanning the lake further down on the left. Also the green-topped trees over by the entrance to the Park and the towering building of Abbey House away down in Baker Street with the red London Transport buses sweeping past in a continuous flow of traffic on their way to Oxford Street. Joey's eyes stopped momentarily to check the time on the large outside clock high at the top of Abbey House. Twenty minutes past one. Time for him to go.

He got to his feet, brushed himself down. He glanced over toward the fence to his left, noticing more people there now than when he first arrived. Mostly women sitting in deck chairs sunning themselves. One of them, he observed, was clad only in a bikini, as she lay stretched out on the grass, her beautiful curved body on display for all to witness. Joey's gaze lingered awhile, appreciating this spectacle before moving to a small group of persons sitting in a circle near to the edge of the lake eating sandwiches. Office workers, probably, enjoying a lunch break from their Banks, Building Societies, Travel Agencies, etc.; that were situated down in the busy hustle and bustle of Baker Street, he thought.

He made his way out onto the pathway and walked slowly down toward the bridge. Flower- beds to his left stretched out in front of him, filling the air with sweet-smelling fragrance. A brightly coloured butterfly fluttered above his head, accompanying him on his walk for a while, then finally came to rest amid the mass of colour amongst the flowers and was lost from sight. At intervals along the pathway wooden seats were positioned, looking out onto the lake. At this hour of the day nearly all were taken, the occupants sitting reading newspapers, feeding the birds, or just relaxing.

A skiff swept swiftly by in the water, a small dumpy man wearing white shorts and vest, expertly manoeuvring the craft smoothly along, the seat of the boat sliding to and fro with his movements. Joey watched as he went up under the bridge and out of sight in the bright sunlight. Crossing the bridge himself, he came upon a large gathering of ducks that were being fed portions of bread from a paper bag by an old woman. He stopped to watch. The old lady looked up at him and smiled, while the birds busied themselves about her, not wanting to miss out on a meal being so kindly offered them by this kind Samaritan. Joey suddenly felt a welcoming calmness surge through him, a rare emotion he so sadly missed these days. He could only put it down to his present surrounds, having always liked this part of the world, especially Regent's Park in particular. His last visit, he remembered, was way back after leaving Lord's one afternoon in late September to give some serious thought as to what he should do with his life now that he realized a career in professional cricket was hardly likely to materialize for him. Good as he was at the game, he knew he couldn't quite compare with the very high standard being set by those select few players who were under consideration by Middlesex County Cricket Club for future positions on their staff. With reluctance, he decided to relinquish any notions he might have of becoming a professional cricketer. So, here he was again - back where he had started.

He looked down at the noisy ducks, wondering to himself where his present life was leading him? His current situation appeared to be somewhat out of control, leaving him powerless to change its course. Whatever will be, will be, and seemed to be his motto at the present moment. Who would have thought that a week ago he would be standing here in Regent's Park, having gone AWOL from the Air Force, charged with assaulting a WAAF officer and striking an NCO? It didn't make sense really. Or did it?

A car horn sounded out on the busy road encompassing the Park. He left the Park and crossed over the road, people now, hurrying to and fro, traffic, congesting the busy streets of London.

Chapter 3 Accommodation

After buying some clothes from a shop in Baker Street, Joey collected his bag from the Station Left Luggage Office and walked to the hotel in Gloucester Place.

"Yes, sir?"

He found himself looking over the reception desk at a gent in a neat grey suit complete with red carnation and big cigar.

"I'd like to book a room for a week, please," Joey said, dropping his bag on the floor.

The man looked him up and down suspiciously. He was without a jacket or tie - casually dressed in a pair of slacks, a pink shirt, a blue, sleeveless pullover and a pair of sandals. To make matters worse, there was a big green stain on his trouser knee from where he'd tangled with the bull that morning.

The neatly suited gent frowned, took the cigar from his mouth and blew a cloud of smoke across the lobby.

"I have stayed here before," Joey got in quickly.

"Really, sir?"

"Yes. Four years ago. I was playing cricket just round the corner. For Middlesex. At Lord's" Now pick the bones out of that, he thought.

"What name, is it, sir?"

"Webster. Joey Webster."

The name meant nothing but the credentials worked. He stuck the cigar back in his mouth and pushed the register across the desk.

"Room number one is vacant, Mr. Webster. Sign here, please."

Joey scribbled his signature in the book for him. Opposite 'NAME' where it said 'ADDRESS', he wrote RAF. And as soon as he'd written it he wished he hadn't, because it struck him right away that he could be lumbering himself. Then he thought, to hell with it.

"On a spot of leave, are we, Mr. Webster?" The gent examined Joey's credentials carefully.

"That's right," Joey lied with conviction. "I might decide to stay longer if that's okay?"

"Of course, sir."

"Good."

"Enjoy your stay with us, Mr. Webster." He took a key off a hook and handed it to Joey.

"First on the left at the top of the stairs."

He might have a smart grey suit, a red carnation and a big cigar - but he didn't have a hall porter. Joey picked up his bag.

"Will you require any meals, sir?"

"Just breakfast, that's all."

"The bar is through there if you should want a drink anytime."

He followed his gaze and noticed a middle-aged couple sitting up at the bar drinking.

"Thank you, Mr. Webster."

"Thank you," said Joey, and began climbing the stairs.

He quickly found his room, it coincidentally being the same one he'd used on his previous visit. Little did he know then that he would be occupying it again now under these present circumstances. He unlocked the door. It looked just the same inside, with the small single bed up against the wall in the center of the room, the bedside table lamp to the right of it; a brightly coloured carpet still spreading the floor, and the wardrobe to the left with the large wicker chair positioned by it. It was a nice comfortable room, and Joey felt immediately at home there. He closed the door, threw his holdall on the bed, walked over to the small window where he looked out onto the rooftops of the buildings opposite. Below, a cobble stoned yard stretched out in front of some white-walled garages. A pleasant, secluded room away from everybody, Joey thought. It would suit him admirably.

He unpacked his few belongings and put them away tidily in the drawers and wardrobe, then went along to the bathroom outside in the corridor for a shave and a good soak in a hot bath.

Refreshed, he returned to his room to put on some clean underwear, socks, shirt, and his pair of new trousers. Then he lay on top of the bed reading Ernest Hemingway's book The Old Man and the Sea that he'd purchased earlier. He decided to buy this after having recalled taking part in a discussion one night in the bar back at camp with a squadron leader, a former war time pilot who got to talking about life in general and said how much he greatly admired this American writer, and recommended Joey should read some of his works. Joey had always been an avid reader, so when he spotted this one on display at the station bookstall, he thought he would give it a try to see what the author had to offer. After only reading the first chapter he knew what the officer had meant by stating what a great writer Hemingway was. Joey had never read anything quite like it before and knew he wouldn't be satisfied until he had finished the book; yet felt at the same time that he must digest it only in small doses. He was like that. If, like this novel, a thing was good, he would prolong its completion by holding on to that goodness for as long as possible. He could compare it rather like a good innings in the game of cricket. You knew the days when you were playing well, and as you progressed you built your score, knowing it would be a respectable one, and so you made it last; because you never really knew when one of a similar nature was going to be. Life's like that, he supposed. The times when the good was there were the times you remembered most.

"That's enough thought for one day," he said out loud, dog-earing the page he'd got to in the book, placing it on the table next to him, springing to his feet. "Food is what's needed at this precise moment."

He glanced round the room, made sure he'd got his key, and then went out, closing the door after him. He descended the stairs, passed through the lobby and bounced down the hotel steps into the bright sunshine outside in the street.

"It's good to be alive!" he sighed joyfully, striding out in the direction of Baker Street.

He came along the road, a continuous stream of traffic crawling by in both directions, signal lights flashing at the crossroads a hundred yards or so away where the Marylebone road cut across Baker Street. The hot sun beat down on the white pavements busy with pedestrians marching to and fro along them. It never ceased to amaze Joey that no matter what time of day in London, there were always hordes of people everywhere. Of all nationalities, all types of dress. He liked to observe them, guessing which part of the world they might be from, what their individual roles in life were. As he passed by a huge block of flats that rose up into the clear blue sky above, he couldn't help wonder who its occupants were and what they did for a living. He imagined them to be all fairly well off as it must cost a fortune to actually own or rent these apartments right here in the heart of London town.

Then he suddenly remembered that he did in fact know of one individual living there after spotting him a few times in the past entering these premises, this person being a well-known cricket writer and music critic for a daily newspaper and whom Joey had often seen frequenting Lord's Cricket Ground and also taking strolls through Regent's Park with an umbrella on his arm and a cigarette protruding from the corner of his mouth in a rather elegant looking, white-boned cigarette holder. The man had the reputation of being one of the finest writers on the game of cricket, and was well respected by all followers of the game. He was a regular visitor to the Park and could be seen walking or sitting there whenever time allowed him this pastime away from the game he loved so much. Probably gathering his thoughts together to comment on the state of play between Middlesex and Yorkshire that he would later write up for The Telegraph for the benefit of his cricketing connoisseurs to read the following morning at their breakfast tables up and down the country. If not this, then perhaps a column commenting on an Elgar cello concerto performed the night previous in the Albert Hall by an up and coming artist new to these shores on a welcomed visit from America.

All these thoughts concerning other people made Joey wonder in which direction his present life was headed at the moment? He had to admit that what he was doing was certainly much better fun than being stuck behind the officer's mess bar back at camp anyway, and came to the conclusion that it was just an interim period for him and would enjoy it while it lasted.

He halted outside a restaurant by the traffic lights. He would take a light snack before venturing along to Lord's, where, he had gleaned from the hotel newspaper earlier, Eton were playing Harrow in their annual cricket match together. The thought of slumming with the gentry from these two renowned historical schools excited him.

The restaurant was spacious inside, with numerous clientele dotted about the place. A young, dark-skinned waiter greeted him and showed him to a table by the window, handing him the menu.

"Just some tea. . . and a poached egg on toast, please!" Joey ordered after some deliberation, getting a certain amount of pleasure in being waited on for a change.

"Thank you, sir!" said the smiling waiter, flashing his white teeth at Joey.

The snack would keep him going until later, he thought to himself, when he could then have something more substantial.

He enjoyed the snack very much and followed it by drinking two cups of excellent tea. Then he sat smoking a cigarette, idly thinking of nothing in particular, and, above all, thoroughly dismissing all thoughts of the Royal Air Force from his mind. Ironically, though, at that precise moment a rather tall, moustached gent wearing the uniform of an RAF officer walked into the restaurant and sat himself down at a table opposite. A squadron leader owning a blotchy-red face registered no recognition as far as Joey was concerned; but even so, with his presence making him feel extremely uncomfortable and having a present dislike for RAF officers, Joey decided to settle up his bill with the polite, young waiter, and leave.

Outside in the street again, he turned left and headed off in the direction of Regent's Park, deciding to walk the short distance up to Lord's. He strolled nonchalantly along in front of the occupied seats close to the edge of the lake upon entering the Park again, the trees very green in appearance, and the clean, fresh air sweet smelling. He took a deep breath, filling his lungs with this sweetness, eager to make the most of his time spent here and to remember it long after it had gone.

An attractive looking nanny pushing a pram passed him by with two small children following close behind twirling skipping ropes and screeching with laughter. An unshaven old man wearing large boots and a pair of trousers with a hole in one knee suddenly appeared from behind a tree and began rummaging around in one of the litter baskets for anything that might be of use to him. These two images brought home to Joey the contrasting realities between the rich and affluent of society and the poor and destitute here in the capital. But then, wasn't this the same picture throughout all the capitals of the world if the truth be known?

Funny really, thought Joey. Here we all are in this Park, each of us going our own separate ways with our own private thoughts, and wondering where the tramp slept at nights was Joey's. This weather, he was all right; but he must get bloody cold during the winter months.

The tramp found nothing of value in the bin, so continued on his weary way, a dirty old bag slung over his shoulder. Joey felt really tempted to run after him and slip the price of a meal in his hand. But the urge just as soon left him, and the old boy was very quickly forgotten.

He arrived at the children's boat pond at the top end of the Park. Shrieks of laughter came from the youngsters as they manoeuvred their gaily-coloured craft along in the water. A worker attired in long rubber leggings waded through the water, disentangling various boats that had gotten into trouble.

Joey stood watching the children innocently enjoying themselves for a while before walking out of the Park and back onto the road that would lead him to Lord's Cricket Ground.

Chapter 4 Eton and Harrow at Lord's

"Watcha, Joey! 'Ow's it goin'?"

"Fine, thanks, Sid. Still here then?"

"Part of the furnicha now, lad."

"All right if I sneak in, Sid?"

"Course you can, Joey. Wot you up to these days, young 'un?"

"Signed on in the RAF, didn't I?"

"Get away – yer never did. . ?"

He made his way into Lord's Cricket Ground and headed in the direction of the Tavern Bar. It certainly was handy having old Sid on duty at the Grace Gate through which he had just passed. The old boy had worked there for as long as Joey could remember and he had often enjoyed listening to him reminisce about past professionals of the game who had started out on their careers at Lord's just as he had a few years back. The Grace Gate wouldn't be the same without the presence of this likeable veteran.

Joey pushed through the milling crowd gathered in front of the Tavern to order himself a beer. He then took his drink and sat in a vacant seat to view the cricket over the tops of the traditional, picturesque carriages that were always a part of this particular match and positioned in a row on the lush, green grass in front of the Tavern fence. An excited hum of conversation filled the air, and a mass of colour from the many elegant hats and dresses worn by the women of society greeted the eye of the beholder. Gents in top hats and tails also gathered for the occasion of this annual cricket match between these two renowned upper class schools.

Joey glanced up at the main scoreboard opposite. Harrow were 178 for the loss of six wickets with the number four batsman having scored ninety-three of these. A ripple of applause carried round the ground as this young man late cut a delivery from the bowler at the Nursery End down in front of them at the Tavern for one run.

"Good shot!" someone from on top of the coach in front of Joey complimented this delicate stroke from the scorer.

"Here's your drink, Charles!" another person spoke, whose job, it appeared, was to keep supplying the coach-load of people with food and drink. This particular gent was now in the process of opening a bottle of champagne, which he took from a hamper resting on the knees of other occupants up on the coach. Portions of chicken also appeared from this tuck-box, outstretched hands reaching up through the open windows from inside the carriage to capture this food, to pass empty glasses aloft for fresh refills.

A tremendous roar from the crowd suddenly burst forth as the number- four batsman hit an almighty six straight into the pavilion to complete his century, a row of pigeons down on the grass by the Mound stand, hurriedly rising into the air, their wings flapping vigorously as they made their way up onto the roof of this enclosure.

"Jumpin' Jove's!" the champagne-gent in the coach sang out, the cork from his bottle, exploding, shooting out over the heads of his colleagues below. Someone else close by screamed with delight at this added attraction, while the chap on the carriage sprang to his feet, filled his glass to the brim with bubbly, and offered a toast to the celebrity out on the cricket field for his very fine achievement. "Oh, well played, sir!"

Then everyone went wild, with champagne corks popping all over the place.

How the other bloody half live, thought Joey, finishing his beer and returning to the bar for a refill so as to join in with their high spirits. They could keep their rotten champagne though. He would stick to his beer.

As he was getting a drink a fair-haired, good-looking woman came up to the bar. "Excuse me," she addressed him very politely, before asking: "Do you know if they sell
cigarettes here?"

He was surprised to find she was not wearing a hat. After witnessing such a variety of them on display everywhere it didn't seem quite right to be suddenly confronted by a member of the fairer sex without one. Come to think of it, he observed there weren't all that many hatless blokes around either. It made him feel most conspicuous standing there dressed as he was for this particular occasion.

"I'm afraid they don't, but there's a confectioners just round the corner from here that does," he kindly informed her.

"I see," she said with a note of sadness in her voice as she began to walk slowly away.

Joey felt in his shirt pocket for his cigarettes. "Here!" he called after her. "Do have one of mine."

She glanced over her shoulder at him, and then strolled back to rejoin him. "That's very kind of you."

"My pleasure," he assured her, feeling in need of company, especially an attractive woman's. "Are you here on your own then?" He hoped she wouldn't think him impertinent.

"Yes, I am in a way," she smiled at him sweetly.

Maybe Joey was mistaken in thinking she wasn't with one of those top-hatted toffs?

"You see – the people I work for invited me along for the day."

Joey paused for a moment before venturing to ask further questions. He lit both their cigarettes upon which she smiled at him once again, presenting a well-shaped mouth with small dimples at the corners.

"Are you enjoying your visit here?" he then asked.

"Yes, very much, although I'm finding it rather embarrassing as I don't know all that many people."

"I know the feeling."

"Are you with anyone?" she enquired with an inquisitive look, raising an eyebrow. She certainly was an attractive woman, Joey observed, with fair hair and bright blue eyes. Her teeth were beautifully white, and she had a very good figure.

Joey sipped his beer, a feeling of excitement mounting inside him because of her presence. "No, I'm entirely on my own," he confessed to her.

"You are obviously a cricket lover then?"

"Yes, I am. I even worked here at Lord's a few years ago."

"Really? How interesting for you."

"Yes, I had dreams of becoming a professional cricketer in those days. They didn't work out though."

"What a pity."

"Yes, it was really. But there we are. Things in life don't always go according to plan, do they?" He thought the time now appropriate for introductions. "My name is Joey, by the way."

"It's nice to meet you, Joey," she said to him with warmth and friendliness. "I'm Lesley."

A shout went up from the crowd as the century-making batsman was out cleaned bowled.

"What's all the excitement about?" Lesley asked.

"The chap who made all the runs is out," Joey explained to her, both of them looking out at the cricket through the opening by the bar, the crowd applauding this particular player appreciably as he made his way up the pavilion steps, the next incoming batsman passing him by on his way out to the wicket.

Joey suddenly realized that Lesley was without a glass in her hand. "I'm so sorry. . ." he apologized. . . "would you like a drink?"

"That's very nice of you, Joey. Thank you; I'd like a nice gin and tonic, please."

Here we go again, thought Joey, remembering the disastrous events and consequences following the last mother's ruin consumer he'd drunk with. What on earth would be in store for him this time? he wondered with a certain amount of apprehension.

He got Lesley a drink and another for himself and they went together to sit in the Stand to watch the cricket.

"I suppose you work here in London, do you, Lesley?"

"Yes, down in Harley Street actualy," his new acquaintance informed him, sipping her iced drink.

"Oh! Cream of the medical profession, eh?"

"I wouldn't really know about that. You see, I'm just a working doctor's receptionist, that's all."

"Interesting work, is it?"

"I find it is, yes. I have my own room and the people I work for are extremely nice." She sampled some more of her drink. "What is it you do for a living now, Joey?"

For the second time that day he lied about the same question concerning part of its reply.

"I'm in the RAF," he confided to her, straight-faced. "On a spot of leave at the moment before returning for demobilization."

"Then what. . ?"

"I'm not sure at the moment." He suddenly felt the need to confide in Lesley, but was frightened to tell her the whole truth regarding his present circumstances lest he should jeopardize their already existing ease with one another at this early stage of their relationship together. He continued their discussion by asking her: "Is your doctor employer here today, Lesley?"

"Yes, with his wife, both suitably dressed for the occasion, I might add. I believe he's an old Etonian or something."

A champagne cork exploded in front of them, and a tall, thin toff donned in the appropriate attire suddenly stood before them on the grass. "Oh, there you are, Miss Williams!" he exclaimed to Lesley, a huge cigar thrust between the fingers of his right hand, his long nose twitching nervously. "I thought we'd jolly-well lost you, m' dear."

"No, no, I'm perfectly safe, thank you, Doctor," Lesley assured the man, turning to smile at Joey with some embarrassment on her part, he detected. "This kind young gentleman came to my rescue. This is Doctor Duncan, Joey. Doctor, I'd like you to meet. . ."

". . .Webster! Joey Webster!" he interjected, wanting to get the necessary introductory formalities over with in a hurry, having no desire to make known his identity to all and sundry at this early stage of his absence from the RAF.

"How do you do, Mr. Webster," the gent greeted him, his nose twitching furiously as he pushed his cigar into his mouth before offering Joey a firm hand to shake, giving him the once over as he did so.

"Joey's in the Royal Air Force," Lesley then made known his secret to the doctor.

Not that there was much he could do to prevent it. Endeavouring to do so would probably only draw suspicion to himself. He decided he would just have to go along with it.

"Really, ol' boy? Navy man myself, yer know." He removed the cigar from his mouth again, his small, bright eyes seeming to approve of Joey. "Care to join us, Mr. Webster?"

Joey hesitated for a moment before answering the man, the doctor swaying on his feet slightly as he stood there looking remarkably like a tailors dummy, his face definitely resembling one, shiny and of a wax appearance. His grey top hat perched on his head added to this impression.

"I – I wouldn't want to intrude," Joey mumbled finally.

"Jolly-well won't be, ol' boy," the doctor assured him, removing his topper and wiping his brow with the back of his hand. "Phew! It's warm."

"A lovely day for the occasion, Doctor," Lesley commented, sipping her drink.

"Wonderful! Now do come along you two and join the rest of us, there's good sports. Just make yourself at home."

The Harley Street man led them over to a coach where Joey was introduced to the doctor's wife. "Nice to meet you, young man!" this lady spoke to him slowly and clearly, offering him her limp hand, whilst in the other a glass of champagne hung delicately between her long fingers.

"That's David up on top of the coach there," the doctor continued with his formalities. "And next to him is young Margaret. . . and then the blue-eyed Sally. Also Brenda, Stephen and Tony."

Joey smiled up at them.

"Hello! Joey," a happy welcome greeted him from above.

"Have some bubbly, ol' sport!" David cried, passing down a tulip-shaped glass filled to the brim with champagne.

"Don't forget Miss Williams!" the doctor's wife shouted to them, smiling, but with her face wearing a sour expression despite this, Joey noticed.

Another glass made its way down, Lesley plucking it from an outstretched hand on route

"The others you can see inside the carriage are Harold, William, Susan and Jean," the doctor droned on, puffing away on his cigar.

Smiling faces peered out at Joey through open windows.

"Joey's in the Royal Air Force," the doctor divulged to his colleagues. Then, amidst applause from the crowd who were appreciating a well-timed stroke from the new batsman that sent the ball hurrying to the boundary for four runs, exclaimed: "Jolly good shot, sir1"

"Damned fine service, too, if I may say so, dear boy!" someone commented from inside the coach.

"What is it you actually do in the RAF, ol' man?" another asked.

"I'm a Corporal and look after the Officers Mess bar!" Joey announced with a certain amount of pride.

"I say – what absolutely marvellous fun that must be for you," one of the ladies suggested with a snigger.

"It does have its moments, darlin'" Joey couldn't help retaliating. Cocky bitch!

"Extremely hard work, I should imagine," added Lesley kindly.

He sampled their champagne. It tasted very dry and reminded him of the last time he'd consumed wine of this nature, which was at an officer's party one night back at the mess. If only sergeant Cummins could see him now, he thought with a wry smile on his face.

"Joey played professional cricket here at Lord's before joining the Air Force," Lesley offered this added piece of information for the doctor's benefit, obviously feeling that he needed more credence regarding his station in life to satisfy his acceptance with them all.

"Really?" exclaimed the surprised doctor at this statement from his receptionist. "I say, ol' boy, is this true?"

"Yes, I was engaged here on the cricket staff for a while," Joey willingly explained, making him feel not quite so bloody inferior fraternizing with this particular lot.

"Did you hear that, Tony, ol' chap?"

"Hear what, Duncan?" a thin-faced, spectacled gent, complete with monkey-suit, enquired.

"Our Corporal here's a cricketer, didn't yer know? Was on the Middlesex staff before entering the armed forces?"

"Weally?"

Joey glanced up at their lisping friend who was now making his way down from the coach above.

"Ready for some more champers anyone?" the drinks man cried from on high on top of the coach.

Both Joey and Lesley finished their bubbly and passed their empty glasses aloft, the pair of them smiling joyfully. To them, it was like being in another world really.

"Playing any cwicket at the moment, Joey?" Tony questioned him with an enthusiasm gained from having gleaned information of Joey's prowess in the game.

"Just for the station team back at camp, that's all," Joey replied.

"Two glasses of the best coming down!" the drinks man shouted enthusiastically.

He reached up for them.

"Any plans for when you leave the RAF?" asked the doctor, his nose twitching.

"No, not really."

"We have a good cwicket club," Tony lisped quietly.

"Jolly-well do with someone like you in the side," the doctor added. The crowd applauded a boundary being struck.

"On leave at the moment, you say," questioned Tony further.

"Yes, that's right." Joey sampled more of the champagne, feeling excited about what was happening to him on his first day away from camp, also of the company he found himself in, and of Lesley now smiling at him from behind her wine glass, dimples and all.

"Pop along the club tomowow – you might get a game?" Tony hinted.

"Better still – come to the party this evening," added the doctor. "Arthur's throwing a barbecue back at his place."

"Have you not met him before?"

"No."

"He'll be here soon," the doctor enlightened him. "Where in London are you staying?"

"At a place in Baker Street."

"That's no problem then. The wife and I can drop you off that way later, if you like."

The doctor's wife glared menacingly at her husband, but added nothing to the conversation.

Joey was feeling quite pleased with the way things were turning out for him. Who on earth would have guessed this morning that he would be mixing with the likes of this lot! And him, a busted corporal at that! He certainly liked the doctor's receptionist though. She, compared with the present company, was in the same class as him really. But then, what the hell did it matter anyway?

"How are you enjoying your first visit to Lord's Cricket Ground, Miss Williams?" the doctor's wife asked her husband's employee, a cigarette protruding from a long cigarette holder that she was holding delicately in her gloved right hand.

"Very much so, thank you, Mrs. Duncan," Lesley answered timidly, almost as if she was afraid to actually say so.

"I'm not all that keen on cricket myself. I know I probably shouldn't make such an outrageous statement in front of you, Mr. Webster. . ."

"Everyone to their own taste," Joey reacted to her comment with the contempt it deserved, wondering to himself why this particular lady looked so continually unhappy all of the time. After all, she was undoubtedly filthy rich and able to afford all the pleasures and luxuries of life. So, why so miserable? An attractive, middle-aged lady with a fine figure, yet she gave one the impression that all was not well with her life.

"I much prefer watching a game of tennis really," she sneered, puffing on her cigarette.

Balls to you, too! thought Joey to himself. Miserable old bat!

"I'm also fond of tennis," Lesley came to her support, obviously wanting to keep on the right side of her. "Do you play the game, Mrs. Duncan?"

"Good gracious, no! I used to once upon a time. I leave that sort of thing to the youngsters now. Rather like most other things these days I'm afraid."

"My good wife thinks she is past it, ol' boy," the doctor intervened, addressing Joey and lighting up a fresh cigar. "You see – I can't jolly-well convince her that I honestly believe she looks as young and as attractive now as when we first met."

"She's absolutely adowable in my opinion," Tony complimented her, smiling, then pushing his spectacles further up the bridge of his rather protruding nose.

"Ah! You men – you're all the same," exclaimed the lady in question, waving her cigarette and holder about in the air. "It's perfectly all right for you. A few grey hairs and a potbelly is all you acquire with the advancing years. You can't possibly imagine what it's like for a woman."

"Oh, come-come, dear!" the doctor addressed his wife rather sternly. "Don't go and ruin the jolly-ol' day for us now. Relax. . .enjoy yourself."

The lady of society glared at her husband for a moment, then answered angrily: "Damn you, Charles! I shall bloody well enjoy myself then! Just you see if I don't!"

"Good for you! Mary. Let your hair down, why don't you?" the drinks man encouraged her from above.

"And don't hog all the booze up there you, either!" she ordered him. "You can pass that bottle of bubbly down for starters!"

A bottle of the stuff made its way to her, the disgruntled lady polishing off the remains of her existing drink and passing her empty glass for Lesley to hold while she wedged her cigarette holder firmly in the corner of her mouth to enable her hands freedom of movement.

"Would you care to join me?" she asked Tony in a very hostile and commanding manner.

"I. . .I'm all wight, thanks, Mawee," he stammered hesitantly, obviously not wishing to upset further her present agitated mood.

"Nonsense!" she hissed, pouring herself a fresh drink. "For goodness sake! Why don't you let your hair down for a change? Your wife's not here, is she?"

"I'm all wight, Mawee, honestly," Tony insisted, standing his ground stubbornly.

"Come along then, Miss Williams! You join me! And you! Mr. Webster. Do have some of this." She topped up their glasses, then turned to face Tony again. "Want to know something, Mr. Webster? Our Tony here tries to make people believe that he doesn't care for drink. But it just isn't true, is it, Tony, dear?"

Tony pretended he was watching the cricket.

Mary, despite her accusations against him, filled his glass to the brim with champagne. "You see – he's so terribly afraid that his charming wife will catch him in the act of doing so one day and discover his wretched secret."

"That'll jolly-well do now, Mary," her husband intervened to chastise her rude behaviour toward Tony.

She gulped down her drink, swayed on her feet, and then snapped: "Oh, do shut up, Charles!"

What looked like developing into an embarrassing situation was avoided by the sudden cry from the drinks man on the coach above. "Look who's arrived everybody?"

A small, rather plump, middle-aged man sporting a bush-handlebar moustache appeared on the scene, pushing his way through the crowd.

"Arthur!" a chorus of voices greeted him.

"Greetings everyone!" this new arrival reciprocated as he began hobnobbing with friends, his face having caught the afternoon sun and bright red in colour. "Gosh! I certainly need a drink."

A drink was handed to him, and, after politely kissing Mary on the cheek, then commenced to enjoy a glass of champagne, his beady eyes darting looks here and there before finally coming to rest on Joey's.

"This is Mr. Webster, Arthur," the doctor introduced him to the man. "Joey, I'd like you to meet Arthur Bryant."

"Hello!" said Joey, offering the gent his hand.

"Joey's in the W-WAF," Tony informed their new guest.

"What's more, he's a fine cricketer," the doctor added. "Used to play for Middlesex!"

"Really?" Arthur enquired with avid interest, a genuine smile breaking across his beetroot coloured face that revealed a set of small, white teeth beneath his walrus moustache.

"We'd like him to play with us," said Tony, sipping his drink slowly, darting the doctor's wife a hurried, almost frightened look.

"We could certainly do with someone like you in our side, young man," Arthur stated, finishing off his drink. "Gosh! I needed that. I trust you blessed lot haven't consumed all the bubbly?"

"Don't fret, Arthur, there's plenty more left," the drinks man confirmed.

"That's good." He looked across at Joey. "Coming along to the party later, Mr. Webster?"

"Thanks, I'd like to," Joey told him, thoroughly enjoying his glass of champers.

Another bottle of Moet & Chandon made its way down to the fold gathered on the grass, Arthur Bryant expertly opening it, the ladies screaming with delight as the contents exploded into a fountain of white foam. "Drink up everyone!" he shouted excitedly. "How's the cricket going, by the way?"

"Looks like it's developing into a drawn game," the doctor declared, holding up an empty glass for replenishment.

"How's that lovely wife of yours today, Charles?" Arthur asked, offering a warm smile to the lady in question.

"You jolly-well better ask Tony," the doctor advised him abruptly.

"Oh dear – have you two been rowing again?"

"No, of course we jolly-well haven't then," Mary, lying to her back teeth, mimicked the impertinent Arthur.

Joey felt Lesley tugging his sleeve. "Are you all right?" she asked him quietly.

"I'm fine, thanks."

"They seem to have taken to you, don't they?"

"Do you think so?"

"What about this party – are you interested?"

"Will you be going?"

"Only if you are."

Joey had the feeling that Lesley had undoubtedly taken to him also, as indeed he had to her, and he felt good about it. "Then we'll go together, shall we?"

As predicted, the cricket match ended in a draw. Not that anyone paid any particular attention to this result. It seemed to be only a secondary concern to those whom Joey had become acquainted with during the course of the afternoon. At least, that was the impression he was left with as the white-clad players trooped off the field at the close of play, as only one or two of the folk perched on top of the coach even bothered to applaud their efforts.

"I think we should give this a miss next year, Charles," Mary suggested to her husband disdainfully. "Perhaps we could watch the tennis at Wimbledon for a change?"

"Have you not enjoyed your day out then, Mary, dear?" Arthur enquired with inquisitiveness, his face crimson, and his moustache twitching.

The lady did not respond to this obvious jibe from the gentleman in question, concentrating instead on the serious business of consuming as much alcohol as was humanly possible for her to do so without making herself extremely ill in the process.

Then Arthur, in a loud and audible voice, announced to all concerned: "Time for the party everyone!"

"Hurrah!" an excited cheer went up from the revellers.

"I'm afraid I shh..ant be going to the party," Mary informed Arthur above all the commotion, her speech somewhat affected by the wine.

He looked at her in disbelief for a moment, unable to grasp the fact that she was about to forgo a free food and drinks evening for probably the first time in all the years of her socializing life. "Why ever not, my dear?"

"Because I'm sloshh..ed, thashh why!"

"You'll be all right, dear," the doctor tried to reassure his wife.

"No I dam well won't, and you know it. I'll be shh..ick ashh a dog if I ashh much ashh look at another bloody drink."

"Don't go and ruin the party for us, dear."

"Shh..ant ruin and bloody party for no one. Take me home, Charl..shh! I want to go home, do you hear? You can go along to the party on your own."

"But what about Miss Williams and her friend, Mr. Webster. . ?"

Mary remained silent, her drowsy eyes half closed, as she just stood there almost asleep on her feet.

"Be a good fellow and take her home, Charles," Arthur stamped his authority on proceedings with a firm voice. "I'll take care of our friends here."

Charles, obviously not wanting his wife to cause any further embarrassment to their friends, made a hurried exit from the scene with her, she, none to steady on her feet.

"What, in God's name, has got into her?" Arthur questioned Tony after their departure, seeking, no doubt, an explanation for Mrs. Duncan's outrageous behaviour.

"I'm afraid Mawee's not been too well today," Tony offered a rather feeble excuse for Mrs. Duncan's conduct.

"Having the same trouble, is she?"

"I weally wouldn't know about that, I'm afwaid."

Standing next to Lesley and listening to this conversation, Joey came to the obvious conclusion that things weren't quite as they should be between the good doctor and his rather melodramatic wife.

With this thought in his mind, Arthur then proceeded to lead them to his parked car over at the far end of the ground.

Chapter 5 The Party

A large, silver-grey Rolls Royce - registration number AB1 - was the sleek looking vehicle that he found himself sitting comfortable in the back of as it slid out of Lord's Cricket Ground and up St.John's Wood Road with the red-faced Arthur Bryant perched in front behind the wheel.

Joey luxuriated in his soft, spacious seat with legs outstretched, Lesley, next to him, in a likewise position. Could this really be happening to him? he wondered in awe at his present circumstances, convinced that he might soon awake from this wild dream he was experiencing.

"On a spot of leave then, are we, Joey?" Arthur then broke the silence to establish the reality of the situation.

He sat with arms folded, feeling very much like a person of special importance as the streamlined automobile purred quietly and contentedly beneath them on its journey. "Yes, that's right," he answered the man, lying yet once again.

"No doubt you'll do some sight-seeing while in London?"

"Yes, probably."

The traffic began to thin out a little, their driver busy concentrating on the road ahead.

Joey looked across at Lesley sitting with her shapely legs crossed beside him. "I suppose you do this sort of thing all the time?" he put to her, smiling.

"No, not at all," she replied, smiling back at him. "Hardly ever, really."

"You certainly choose the right company to enjoy yourself with?"

"I can assure you that it's not always like this."

"Isn't it. . ?"

"No, this is my first day out in ages."

He offered her another one of his cigarettes.

"I never did get any, did I?"

"Just as well. I would never have come to really know you if you had, would I?"

"Yes, that's true. We probably wouldn't be sitting here talking together either?"

The car cruised impressively along on its journey. Every now and again Joey caught sight of their reflection in the Swiss Cottage shop windows, the sun striking the car dazzling-bright as it sank slowly from the sky above the rooftops of the buildings directly ahead of them. It had been a wonderful day. It looked like developing into a good evening also. He began to wonder how things might be back at his camp. If the lads could only see him now, he chuckled quietly to himself. They would have a bloody fit! That's for sure.

Fifteen minutes later they motored down through Harrow on the Hill, journeyed on for another mile or so before turning off left along a gravelled driveway that eventually led them to a rather large looking house.

"You have been here before, of course, Miss Williams," their chauffeur indicated, leaning back in his seat.

"I have, yes, Mr. Bryant," Lesley acknowledged his statement, uncrossing her legs.

The Rolls came to a halt at the top of the driveway in front of a house with two white-painted doors, one of which was open and the other displaying a huge brass knocker that glinted in the fading sunlight.

"Here we are then!" Arthur Bryant informed his two passengers. "Do go right in and make yourselves at home while I put the car in the garage."

Joey got out of the car, hurried round the other side to open the door for Lesley, bowing low as she stepped down from the spacious interior. "Your ladyship!" he greeted her in jest, the car then moving slowly off round to the rear of the house.

"I feel like Cinderella!" Lesley exclaimed good-humoredly, taking hold of his arm and smiling.

"Well, we better enjoy ourselves before midnight strikes, hadn't we?"

Moments later they were to find themselves standing inside the entrance of a marble stoned hallway of the house. An exceptionally thick-carpeted stairway climbed upwards to their immediate left. The sound of voices could be heard coming from behind a half open door at the foot of the stairs to the right.

Joey took a deep breath. "Shall we go in?" he boldly suggested, bravely pushing open the door.

"Good evening!" a woman's voice greeted them from the far end of a room the size of football pitch.

"Good evening!" both Joey and his charming companion replied simultaneously, making their grand entrance.

"Have you by any chance seen that husband of mine on your travels, dearies?"

"He's parking his car, Mrs. Bryant," Lesley informed the lady of this luxurious house.

"Oh, that's good. I thought for a moment he had gone missing or something. Do please come along in, Miss Williams and help yourselves to a drink."

They moved toward a large group of people who were standing in the middle of the room drinking.

"And who, may I ask, is the good looking young man you have on your arm, Miss Williams?" Mrs. Bryant wanted to know.

"His name is Joey Webster, Mrs. Bryant."

"Well, it's a pleasure to meet you, Joey Webster. Now - what would you like to drink?"

He looked at their attractive, expensively dressed, middle-aged hostess, feeling somewhat nervous at suddenly becoming the center of attraction amongst all these upper class people. "I – I'll have a scotch and soda, please!" he finally requested with slight hesitancy. Well, he couldn't very well have asked for a pint of beer now, could he?

"What's you tipple, Miss Williams?"

"Thank you; I'll have the same, Mrs. Duncan."

And that's how it was for the rest of the evening as more guests arrived to join in with the drinking before wandering off to stand in groups or sit in comfortable armchairs to converse with each other on topics of interest. Joey found it all a little embarrassing to begin with, not really knowing anyone; but eventually he began to relax and to actually enjoy being in the company of the so-called well to do in an odd sort of a way.

Then Arthur Bryant appeared on the scene. "Food is about to be served everyone!" he informed his guests in a voice loud enough for them to hear as he stood beside a highly polished grand piano at the far end of the room.

Excited murmurs filled the lounge as a milling crowd slowly began making its way out onto the lawn.

"Come along, you two! No dawdling," Tony addressed Joey and Lesley, this being the first opportunity they'd had of seeing him since leaving Lord's. Accompanying him now was a rather pretty, blue-eyed woman wearing a stunning red, low cut summer dress that showed off her beautiful, large-breasted figure to the fullest. "May I intwoduce my wife, Cawol, to you, Joey."

"How very nice to meet you," a cultured voice greeted Joey with extreme politeness.

"Hello!" He suddenly remembered the doctor's wife's acid remarks concerning this particular woman earlier at the cricket.

"Is it true, Joey, that you were once a professional cricketer?"

He cleared his throat in preparation to offer his best diction at such short notice. "Yeah, that's right, lady," However, his final speech offering fooled nobody, least of all himself, so he decided there would be no more airs and graces on his part when talking with these people whilst in their presence.

"It must have been a marvellous experience for you?" Suddenly, she changed the topic of conversation. "And you, Miss Williams – are you enjoying the day off from your Harley Street duties?"

"Very much so," Lesley answered.

"Let's go and eat, shall we?" Tony suggested, making a move to join the others, who, by now, were assembled outside on the lawn and queuing for their promised meat steaks.

After waiting a few minutes on the patio, where both the Bryant's could be seen busy barbecuing and serving the food, Cinderella and her Prince Charming collected their meal of steak and sizzling mushrooms, rolls and butter, and made their way onto the spacious lawn to sit at one of the many tables dotted about the area. A pond was situated in the middle of the lawn, complete with cascading water fountain, while away to their left, stood a rather elegant summerhouse.

"They really do enjoy the best things in life these people, don't they?" Joey commented, enjoying the food.

"They most certainly do," Lesley agreed. "But I honestly believe that some of them are not as content with their lives as probably you or I, Joey."

When they had finished eating, Joey lit them both a cigarette, then noticed the drinks man from Lord's earlier sitting with a group of lady friends inside the summerhouse who were all busy eating and talking.

"I shouldn't be too envious of them, Joey. Indeed, I know for a fact that the majority of them are extremely unhappy."

He looked around at the numerous folk gathered on the lawn, a hum of conversation filling the warm night air. A line of tall poplar trees stood to attention at the top of the large garden, their leaves quivering in the soft breeze. He spotted Tony and his wife sitting close to the pond's edge. Also the doctor, returned once more to be with his friends after seeing his wife safely home. There were many other faces present, but as of yet, unknown to him.

"You reckon all these toffs on being a right miserable bunch then, do you?" He found Lesley's statement hard to swallow.

"I wouldn't exactly say they were miserable. Unhappy – yes."

"I wonder why that is?"

"Probably because they have most things in life, and having got them are dissatisfied."

Joey glanced over his shoulder at the doctor who was busy engaged in a deep conversation with Arthur Bryant's wife. "What did our host mean back at Lord's by asking Tony whether Mrs. Duncan was still having a problem?"

Lesley deliberated for quite some time before answering his question. "I shouldn't really be telling you this-"

"-But you're going to anyway. . ?"

"Promise me you won't mention this to a soul?"

"I promise, Lesley."

"It-it's just that Mrs. Duncan finds it necessary to have a special back rest at night in bed."

"Nothing wrong in that, is there?"

Lesley cleared her throat. "She and the Doctor only use this device when they want to make love together."

He could see she was obviously embarrassed by having divulged this information to him.

"Consequently, Mrs. Duncan has now developed numerous other complaints deriving from this practice, hasn't she? For one, she thinks she has lost her appeal toward men. She also believes she looks much older than she should for her age and that all her friends will learn of this secret and make her the laughing stock of London."

"I see what you mean." Joey couldn't help but wonder at the strangeness of it all really.

"Swear you won't breathe a word of this to anyone?"

"Scouts honour!"

For the next few minutes they both sat smoking in silence, each of them with their own thoughts with regards to this knowledge concerning the doctor's wife. Joey found it all rather amusing. Farcical, in a way.

"What of that other business with Tony and his wife that Mrs. Duncan ranted on about?"

Lesley knocked the ash from her cigarette.

"Inquisitive old thing, aren't we?"

"I like to know the company I keep, luv!" he joked.

She smiled, making the dimples that Joey found so attractive to appear at the corners of her shapely mouth. "Tony and Carol are an extremely nice couple."

"Are they weally?" He couldn't resist the mimic.

"Although he tries hiding the fact that he's a very heavy drinker. He managed to keep this from his wife for some quite considerable time, but she eventually found him out. Do you know what? She absolutely forbade him to ever touch another drop, and said she would leave him if he did."

"Weally?" he chuckled once again.

"It did the trick. You'll never see Tony drinking while she's around."

He stubbed his cigarette out in the ashtray on the wrought iron, floral-designed garden table. "Does Tony's wife drink herself?"

"Yes, she does."

"Then I don't understand. . ?"

"No, and you never will with these people, Joey."

"I mean – if she's partial to a drop – then why the hell isn't he allowed any?"

Lesley's eyebrows arched above her charming, Wedgewood-blue eyes. "Probably because she's worried he might discover her secret, I suppose."

"Which is. . ?"

"That she's been having an affair with the Doctor!"

"Well! Weally!"

He glanced over at Tony's wife seated at a table close to the pond; her attractive face a blurred image on the other side of the water fountain. "Does Tony know of the affair?"

"Well, of course he knows."

What a state of affairs! "It gets more and more complicated by the minute, doesn't it? Why all the bloody pretence for chrisake?"

"To create a false impression I suppose." Lesley answered.

"What on earth for?"

"Well, as you know, most of this crowd are fairly wealthy and lack for nothing really. The one thing they want is themselves. They've lost that though because of their lifestyles. They put on a big show about pretending to care for each other; but nothing is further from the truth, is it? Hence, all this nonsense between Tony and his wife. She imagines she has advantage over him with regards to his drinking habits, while he believes he's put one over on her with knowledge of her affair. Ironically, the real winner of the contest however is Tony because he's been having an affair with the Doctor's wife, hasn't he?"

"Wouldn't it be easier all round just to divorce each other?" This seemed the perfectly logical solution to both their problems.

"No, that would never do." Lesley appeared to be enjoying her continuing saga. "They don't want all the fuss and bother that would entail. Too much at stake for them to lose with their fine big houses and motorcars and all. No, they just continue going their own ways, each thinking one is happier than the other. But they're far from happy. No trust left between them, you see."

Joyous laughter burst forth from inside the summerhouse, the drinks man rising to his feet to stride out across the lawn, his many lady friends following on behind, giggling like excited schoolgirls. Other guests were now headed in the same direction also.

At this point Tony and his wife joined them at their table. "Enjoy the food?" He peered down at them through his spectacles.

They both gazed up. "Very much, thank you."

"Come inside the house and meet a few of the cwicket team, Joey."

"Yeah, why not," Joey agreed.

They stood up and followed him across the lawn, rubbing shoulders with other guests on the way. The ladies all still looked very elegant in their hats and dresses, while the gents, in contrast, appeared to be only half dressed, having now dispensed with the wearing of their top hats.

Inside the house the Bryant's were busy once again pouring drinks for those who had gathered in the lounge to continue with their socializing.

"A wonderful meal! Arthur," a woman's voice could be heard complimenting the host.

"Excellent!" echoed another.

"Take these drinks, will you, Joey." Tony passed some over on a silver-plated tray.

They stood in a group drinking champagne. Tony, however, resisted the temptation.

"A deliciously tasting steak, don't you think, Joey?" Carol's face seemed a little flushed now that they were inside out of the cool night air.

"Scrumptious!" He had always been a man of few words.

"I trust the Doctor's not been working you too hard, Miss Williams?"

"No, not really." She was hardly likely to say otherwise now, was she?

"Which reminds me – I have something to discuss with Charles. Please excuse me, won't you?"

"Yes, deawest." Tony watched his wife walk off in pursuit of the doctor.

A tall, very thin chap pushed his way through the crowd, an empty glass clutched in his hand. "Tony!" he cried jubilantly. "Not drinking, ol' boy?"

Obviously, Tony's drinking habits were a standing joke with all concerned.

"Keith!" With trepidation, Tony peered over his shoulder at his overzealous companion. "I'd like you to meet Joey here. He was once on the gwound staff at Lowd's. This is Keith, Joey, the captain of ouwah cwicket club."

The skipper shook him vigorously by the hand. "Pleased to meet you, Joey." His greeting was certainly warm and friendly.

Joey had the feeling he was dreaming again. After all, what the hell was he doing here in this bloody great house mixing with this lot?

"We would certainly welcome someone of your calibre in the club, Joey." Keith woke him from this figment of his imagination back to reality once again. "Why don't you look us up some time?"

"I might at that." It could be fun, Joey thought to himself.

He was then introduced to a small, portly man with a walrus moustache and dark, seal like eyes.

"Interesting. . .yes, very interesting," was his only contribution to the conversation upon learning of Joey's cricket history.

"And this is ouwah wicket-keepwa, Tommy Simpkins." Tony was doing well with his introductions. "And Weggie Smith, an extwemely fast bowla."

They all did their utmost to make Joey feel at home and expressed a desire that he should come and play cricket for them sometime.

"Why don't you pop along tomowow," Tony suggested eagerly. "You will most likely get a game. I believe the Pwesident is minus a man in his eleven."

"Yes, all right, I will." The prospect of playing cricket again made him feel excited.

"In case you don't know – the gwound is situated at the top of Hill Woad – the Southbank Cwicket Club. Wight opposite The Noke public house. Established a hundwed yeawas ago. Know of it?"

"Yes, I do, actually." He was beginning to even sound like them now, God help him.

"It's an all-day game. Should be good fun."

Then Frank Sinatra came bouncing out of a hi fi with his Songs For Swingin' Lovers, couples pairing off to dance in the middle of the floor.

It was then also that Joey began to feel somewhat isolated from everyone; coming down to earth you might say with a bump, realizing his true identity and seriously questioning his presence among these people in this luxurious home. He finished drinking his glass of champagne, his mind in a whirl, his eyes seeking for the whereabouts of Lesley, the one person with whom he felt completely at ease; but they could not locate her. Where the hell had she disappeared to suddenly? Without her at his side he was like a fish out of water.

An extremely attractive woman then appeared at his side rather unexpectedly. "Care to dance, young man?" Her request sounded more like a command.

"Why not!" he agreed without hesitation, placing his empty glass on the table, feeling grateful for having someone come to his rescue.

They took to the floor as Sinatra swung into Monterey.

"You must be the young cricketer everyone's talking about?" His smiling partner was blue-eyed, auburn-haired and in her late thirties, with a beautifully shaped body that pressed close to his as they moved round the room.

"I suppose I am." It saved having to introduce himself.

"The Doctor asked me to tell you that he's gone on ahead to Harley Street with Carol and Miss Williams."

"Oh. . ?" Now why have they done that? he wondered, sad at the thought of losing Lesley. Perhaps he might never see her again?

A soft voice in his ear then added: "Don't look so worried, sweetie! I've been asked if I wouldn't mind driving you back to your place."

"I see."

"You don't mind, do you?"

Well, of course he didn't mind. "Left a bit early, didn't they?" No doubt an ulterior motive lay behind this change of plan?

"The Doctor mentioned something about the necessity of seeing his wife. And Carol said she had some business to discuss with the Doctor that couldn't wait." Joey's new acquaintance gazed up into his eyes. "By the way – where are you staying, young man?"

"I'm at a small hotel down in Baker Street." The truth, for a change.

Sinatra was now visiting New York In June, the floor crowded with other couples as they talked and laughed and enjoyed themselves.

"The name's Jenny," his dancing partner introduced herself, her soft cheek close to his, her perfume, sweet-smelling.

"Pleased to meet you, Jenny." He suddenly caught a glimpse of Tony disappearing out through an open door at the far end of the room. "Mine's Joey."

"What do think of the party?"

"Yeah – it's ok."

"RAF boy, aren't you?"

She certainly had done her homework on him, hadn't she? "That's right, although I'm due to leave the service any day now." Their conversation, like everything else, seemed unreal somehow.

"Any immediate plans for the future, Joey?"

"I'm not sure really," he sighed despondently. "In fact, I'm not sure of anything at the moment."

She raised her head from his shoulder to gaze into his eyes. "You'll find your way, don't you worry."

He made no reply to her assurance of his welfare. Who on earth was this woman anyway? And what was he getting himself into with his involvement with her?

Sinatra kept on singing, couples kept on dancing, while he kept on wondering, with this dame's head resting on his shoulder.

He endeavoured to engage her in some small talk. "Hubby not at the party then?"

"No, sweetie!" she whispered rather seductively in his ear. "At this very moment he's sailing the high seas."

"Is that so?" Well, bully for him!

"He's a ship's officer on a passenger liner bound for America."

He sounded like a real Christopher Columbus, didn't he? Not that Joey was particularly interested.

"Yes, so while he's off roaming the spacious seas, I'm left here all on my little own. Not fair, is it, sweetie?" She moved closer still to him, her long fingers caressing the back of his neck. "So, how about if you and I go for a spin in my sports car?"

Joey gulped nervously at her suggestion. "I-I don't mind." Why the hell should he? She was a very good-looking woman.

"We can drive round for a bit to blow the cobwebs from our hair before going back to my place for a nightcap. What do you say to that, sweetie?"

"Sounds fine to me," he agreed to her suggestion unquestioningly.

"You run along and wait for me outside while I go powder my nose."

She slipped away as they reached the far end of the room, and he made his way out of the house without anyone paying much attention. He felt a little guilty in not saying goodnight to the Bryant's and to thank them for the swell nosh.

It was almost dark outside now. Jenny soon joined him, and they made their way through the mass of parked cars to find hers. A sleek. red sports job. After a little manoeuvring, they roared off down the drive in it together, headlights on, illuminating the darkness before them.

Ten minutes later found them both sitting in the lounge of Jenny's place. Her house was considerably smaller than the Bryant's; but nevertheless expensively furnished and very comfortable indeed.

"I've been drinking rather a lot today," he opened the conversation, sipping a whisky that she had poured him from a huge, cut-glass decanter.

She smiled, sitting opposite him. "Have you, sweetie?"

"I made the most of a good thing I suppose."

"Why not indeed?"

"You weren't at the cricket, were you?"

"No, I couldn't make it unfortunately. I hear you spent some time at Lord's?"

"Yes, before joining the RAF."

The conversation ceased momentarily, making him feel ill at ease with this particular woman who had literally kidnapped him to bring him here to her house. Glancing across at his new acquaintance, he noticed her watching him closely which only added to his uncomfortable ness.

"Relax, sweetie!" Her advice to him was uttered almost in a whisper. "I don't frighten you, do I?"

He offered no reply, trying to avoid her eyes that seemed to be in the process of undressing him. Instead, he glanced to his right at a vase of beautiful pink roses that were on display on top of a highly polished grand piano. Do all this bloody rich set have piano's sitting inside their living rooms? he thought to himself with amusement.

"Come and sit over here!" Jenny's seductive words enticed him, patting the arm of her chair.

Joey felt himself rise from the sofa and move toward her. She reached out for his hand, grasped hold of it tightly and pulled him down onto his knees in front of her. She leaned forward, her face close to his, her eyes searching his. Then, cupping his face in her soft hands, she kissed him, passionately, the aroma from her perfume intoxicating him.

And then the bloody telephone rang, shattering the silence, tearing them apart.

"Hell!" Jenny snapped furiously, rising to her feet, leaving him in a humiliating heap on the floor while she went out into the hallway to answer the telephone.

He picked himself up and went to browse at some books on a shelf over by the window.

"I'm terribly sorry, sweetie!" Jenny had entered the room again. "But I'm going to have to ask you to leave." It was not only a form of an apology on her behalf, but also a request for him to make himself scarce. He was beginning to feel more and more bemused by it all.

"That was my husband just on the phone. He's on his way here now."

"But I thought you said he was away sailing the high seas?"

"Yes, he was supposed to be. There's been a change of plans apparently. He's not going to be making the voyage after all."

"I see." Did he bloody hell!

She moved closer to him. "You poor dear. Just when. . .I'm so sorry, sweetie!"

"That's all right. It doesn't matter."

She planted a sympathetic kiss on his cheek as a consolation prize. "Perhaps another time, eh?"

"Yes, perhaps." His pride had been hurt though. "What happens now?"

"I'll drop you off at the station if you like? It's the least I can do under the circumstances."

It was while they were driving to the station that he suddenly thought of him – the husband – poor bastard! Talk about when the cat's a way, the mice will play, eh? These folk didn't seem to have any morals whatsoever in their behaviour towards each other. After all, he had only known this woman an hour at most, and here she was offering to hop in bed with him the moment her husband was away earning the money to keep her in a lifestyle she was accustomed to. He was glad now that the phone had interrupted them when it did.

"Are you terribly disappointed?" Jenny drove the car extremely fast, but safe, the streets comparatively free of traffic at this hour of the night.

"It doesn't matter," Joey replied sharply.

"Do keep in touch."

"I'll do that."

They came to an abrupt halt outside the entrance to the railway station.

"Here we are then." She leant across to open the door for him. "Look me up sometime. Don't forget now?"

"Thanks for the lift." He got out the car. "No, I won't forget." He knew he would though. Time would take care of that. Besides, the whole bloody episode was ridiculous anyway!

Jenny's red sports job roared away, turning left out onto the main road, and then disappeared from view.

He heaved a deep sigh, turned on his heel and began climbing the stone stairway toward the ticket office. "It was fun while it lasted, I suppose," he muttered quietly to himself.

Back in Baker Street, he popped into a Milk Bar for a coffee before returning to his hotel. He sat smoking a cigarette thinking over in his mind the events of that day. And what a day it had been. If that was anything to go by, then what would the rest of his stay in London be like? he wondered.

Chapter 6 The Southbank Cricket Club

Joey got up early next morning, bathed, shaved, dressed himself, and went down to breakfast. The middle-aged couple he had spotted the previous day were the only other people using the dining room, he noticed. He smiled at them as he made his way over to a table positioned in front of a large bay window that looked out onto Gloucester Place. Outside, the sun once again shone gloriously, while traffic zoomed by in the street unceasingly.

A pleasant-faced, elderly waitress entered the room and came and stood by his table.

"A full breakfast, please!" he ordered from her with a smile. "And a pot of tea."

"Thank you, sir!" She returned his smile.

He enjoyed the meal immensely and then sat looking out the window sipping tea whilst smoking his first cigarette of the day. The eventful happenings of the previous day were still fresh in his mind. The red sports job certainly brought a smile to his face, while the thought of not having seen more of Lesley saddened him a little. He would seek out the doctor's phone number and maybe give her a ring later. Perhaps she might like to join him at the Southbank Cricket Club where he planned to visit after finishing his breakfast. He felt excited as the prospect of another interesting day lay before him.

Before leaving the hotel, he went to his room to get some money. He then made his way along to Baker Street Station, with the sun warm and beating down from a cloudless blue sky again. The pavements were crowded with pedestrians, the streets busy with traffic.

Inside the station he found an empty phone booth, pulled the slide doors shut and skipped through the pages of a telephone directory. After locating the Harley Street number he wanted, he quickly wrote it on the back of his cigarette packet, then dialed it. A pause. . .

"Hello! Doctor Duncan's residence." He recognized Lesley's voice immediately.

"Lesley! It's Joey Webster."

"Oh! Hello – how are you?"

"I'm fine. . ."

"You managed to get back to your hotel all right last night then?"

"Yeah – I was offered a lift." He omitted to inform Lesley of the precise details of his extraordinary experience with Jenny relating to this though.

"That's good."

"Tell me – do you have to work today, Lesley?"

"No, I don't. Why?"

"I was wondering whether you would like to join me for a day out. . ?"

His suggestion was met with a brief silence. He could hear the escalator outside the cubicle rolling round and round on its journey up and down the Underground.

"It's very sweet of you to ask, Joey," he heard Lesley's voice speaking to him again, "but I'm afraid I have a hairdressers appointment later. I also have some shopping to do. What had you in mind?"

He cleared his throat, worried for a moment that she might refuse his offer. "I'm going to visit the Southbank Cricket Club – fancy coming along there with me? You also owe me a packet of cigarettes, remember?"

He heard her laugh. "Tell you what – I could meet you there later if you like?"

"I'd like that very much."

"Around four-o-clock..?"

"That'll be fine. You know where the ground is?"

"Yes, I've been there before. I must dash. Thanks for phoning, Joey. See you later."

"Bye, Lesley."

He came out the cubicle and walked over to the ticket office where a tall, well-built West Indian confronted him behind a glass partition. "Return to Harrow-on the Hill, please!" The man, jacketless, with rolled-up shirtsleeves over his dark, muscular arms, wore a bright yellow tie that hung from his neck at half-mast, the top shirt button of which was left unfastened as he looked out at Joey through a small hole in the window. His physique and bearing reminded him of a coloured fast bowler he had once done battle with on the cricket field, both of them having gained enormous respect for each other at the conclusion of this contest together.

"Thank you, sir!" he addressed Joey politely with a smile, a glinting gold tooth and beads of perspiration lining his smooth-skinned forehead.

Joey stepped onto the descending escalator toward the trains. Glass-framed advertisements for ladies stockings, men's wear, and West End cinema attractions, along with numerous other attractions lined the walls. People ascending the escalator opposite rode past, the last of these being a little old lady cradling a small dog lovingly in her arms. As they came in line with Joey, the dog began barking at him. The old gal paid no attention to this, her thin, heavily lined face expressionless as she gazed above her, quite oblivious to the irritating noise her animal was causing the rest of the public. Joey couldn't resist sticking his tongue out at the offending mutt. The dog became even more agitated at this, yapping away more noisily at him. Joey managed to get one more tongue-wag in as he stepped off the escalator at the bottom, the dog continuing on his journey, peering down and still barking angrily at him from above.

"Stupid animal!" he murmured to himself, bounding off up the stairs to his right, bringing him onto a platform where a long, silver train stood waiting to pull out.

Twenty minutes later the train deposited him safely at Harrow-On-The-Hill Station, the well-known church spire piercing the sky high up on the Hill and plainly visible for miles around. He alighted from the train feeling free, happy and contented with the way things had materialized for him since yesterday. Here he was on his way to watch a cricket match, have a few drinks, and later, if things went according to plan, meet a pretty woman. What more could anyone wish for?

He hailed a taxi outside the station and instructed the cabby to take him to Southbank Cricket Club. He enjoyed the ride, the bright sunshine outside, the exuberant feeling of another day about to unfold.

"Grand day, guv?" his driver commented amiably.

"Marvellous!" he agreed.

"Just right for cricket, I reckon?"

"Couldn't be better, could it?"

They journeyed on about a mile before arriving at the Cricket Club, a quaint, picturesque church situated just down the road from it with a gold-numeral clock positioned high on its flint-stoned wall. He'd passed this way many times before, but had never actually visited the Southbank ground. He had played cricket at most of the London clubs since leaving school. This particular one had eluded him somehow. Lime trees in full bud ran in a line the other side of a tall privet hedge all down one side of the ground. A small public house – The Noke - stood opposite the ground just off the main road.

The taxi travelled slowly along a roadway leading up to the cricket pavilion, a notice board with Southbank Cricket Club painted on it positioned at the entrance. To the left of the entrance was a farmhouse and another sign, Southbank Riding School. He noticed a white picket fence in front of the house and the top of a barn roof showing above the house at the rear. An expanse of field with horses and riders galloping freely, some of who were jumping over obstacles spaced out at intervals, stretched away to the left and behind the cricket pavilion.

"Here we are, guv!" The cab driver came to a halt beside the club house where other cars were parked close by off the road behind the fence of the cricket field on the other side of a marked boundary line that showed white on the green, close-cut grass.

He stepped out of the cab, paid his fare and stood looking across at the cricket square where stumps were already in position at either end of the pitch and shining golden in the bright morning sunshine. He saw also the white-painted sightscreens at the far end of the ground standing tall and erect in front of the trees and hedge. He thought the ground rather small in comparison with others he'd been played on in the past. Small, but beautifully set in picturesque surroundings. The ground itself was on a slope that no doubt helped with the drainage during wet weather. It seemed hard to believe that all of this was only a stone's throw away from London. One could easily imagine being right in the heart of the countryside somewhere. He felt safe and very much at ease here. "If Sergeant Cummins could see me now he'd have a bloody fit!" Joey chuckled quietly to himself.

He watched the taxi move off, and then turned to face the pavilion, a small but very impressive looking building constructed entirely from wood with a tin roof. A veranda looked out onto the cricket field, in front of which was a roped-off, grass-verged area with a sign marked Members Enclosure. Colourful deck chairs were arranged here in neat rows with a pathway running down the centre onto the field. Geranium plants, their petals splashes of red in contrast to the green grass, were planted out in cultivated plots of earth in an orderly line behind the deck chairs either side of the path directly below the veranda. Wide windows each side of the pavilion door opened into the building, hung from inside. On the right at the far end of the pavilion was a serving hatch for the bar, around which stood a cluster of people drinking. A scoreboard was situated to the right of the bar on a grass verge the other side of the veranda. Inside the pavilion, the two cricket teams were gathered together with other guests and friends as they stood around talking and drinking. A loud laugh suddenly burst forth, echoing all round the ground, which, even at this hour of the day had attracted some spectators who were dotted about and eagerly waiting for the start of play. An electric clock hung precariously above the pavilion door with its hands pointing at eleven-o-clock precisely.

Joey decided it was time for him to make known his presence to everyone as he made toward the pavilion. A brick building with a sign Tea Hut on display outside it stood to his left by the pathway leading up to the club house. He noticed a group of ladies and a gent inside busy preparing salad lunches for later.

"Good morning!" Tony's wife, Carol, addressed him.

He returned her jovial greeting. "Good morning! Lovely day!"

"Isn't it gorgeous? You'll find Tony in the pavilion."

"Thanks."

He carried on along the pathway.

Chapter 7 Ground Blessing

Joey stepped up on to the long, wooden veranda of the pavilion, feeling slightly nervous as the sound of voices became prominent through the open window on his left.

"Hello! Joey," he heard Tony's voice shout to him above the commotion before appearing in the open doorway to greet him enthusiastically. "How nice of you to make it."

"Yes, I thought I'd come along." Tony's warm welcome deserved acknowledgement.

"Please do come on in and have a dwink."

He followed Tony up to the bar, the pavilion crowded inside with people, some of who were changed into their cricketing attire. Others sported blazers and wore colourful neckties. A haze of smoke from cigars, pipes and cigarettes hung above the heads of everyone.

"What will you have?" Tony had commandeered a rather tall, rosy-cheeked toff dressed in a light summer jacket and an open-necked shirt with a blue and white-specked cravat who was standing behind the small but very well arranged bar.

"A pint of bitter will do fine." It would quench the thirst he was experiencing from yesterdays over indulgence of champagne.

"This is Chawles Bellamy, Joey. He wuns the Club bawa." Tony paused. "I'd like you to meet Joey Webstwa, Chawles – the young Middlesex chap I told you about."

A well-manicured hand extended over the beer pumps toward him, a broad smile spreading across the man's face. "Pleased to make your acquaintance, young man," he spoke softly and with distinction, shaking him firmly by the hand before pulling him up a pint of beer.

Tony paid for his drink. "I'll be back in a minute. I want to speak with the captain."

"I believe Tony's trying to fix you up with a game." Charles Bellamy placed his drink on the counter.

Joey took a good swig of his beer. "But I've no cricket gear with me."

"That won't present a problem – the boys will fix you up with some, I'm sure."

"Are they a man short then?"

"No – I believe he said something about playing twelve a side."

"I see." He hadn't expected a game; but if asked, would feel obliged to play considering how well he had been treated by these people since making their acquaintance yesterday. He would no doubt also enjoy the experience.

He stood up at the bar looking around. He noticed a row of tables lining one side of the wall of the pavilion with chairs stacked on top of them. He also observed some framed photographs of various cricket teams arranged on the walls.

"I understand you were at Lord's, young man?" Charles Bellamy enquired, offering him a cigarette.

"Yes, that's right." He lit the cigarette.

"In the RAF at the moment, I hear?"

"I am, yes."

Joey suddenly felt threatened with this cross-examining by the barrister-type character from behind the bar. He discovered later that the gent was a stockbroker working in the city of London.

"Where are you stationed, Joey?"

He felt like telling the geezer to mind his own bloody business! Politeness, however, prevailed finally in his reply to the question as he endeavoured to hide his resentment toward the man for pursuing this line interrogation. "RAF Ralston."

"Oh! Only just up the road from us then?"

"Yeah, I run the Officer's Mess bar there."

"Really? Us two certainly do have something in common then, don't we?"

"I suppose we do." No doubt his was more a labour of love than of necessity, unlike Joey's.

"It's damned hard work running a successful bar, wouldn't you agree?"

"It most certainly is." Joey wanted desperately to change the subject for reasons best known to himself.

The toff pulled a beer for himself. "Are you from this part of world, Joey?"

A vision of his home and his mother formed immediately in his mind. He wondered what on earth she would think of him mixing with this upper crust lot. He must pay her a visit soon to explain how he had come to be in his present position with them. "I'm from the town of Wufton – just up the road."

"You'll take up playing cricket again in Civvy Street, no doubt?"

"Probably, yeah."

"We have an extremely good cricket club here, you know." He stood playing proudly with his spotted cravat.

Joey peered out through the open window. "You certainly do have a nice ground," he remarked.

"Yes, you'd be surprised how many visitors comment on its quaintness. We are all very fond of it. It is such a charming spot here. Some damned fine Club members here as well. From all walks of life. We even have a Squadron Leader from your outfit playing for us, Joey."

"A Squad – wotsisname...?"

"Cockshott! Charlie Cockshott – do you know him?"

He heaved a sigh. The name didn't ring a bell. And with a name like that, one undoubtedly should have.

"He – he's not playing today, is he?"

"Indeed, he is – never been known to miss the President's match, old Charlie."

Joey didn't like the sound of it. No, not one bit. They were bound to be introduced. Then what? Maybe he shouldn't have come here after all?

Tony re-appeared alongside him at the bar. "What size boots do you use, Joey?" He was waving a pair of spiked ones above his head in the air.

He finished his drink. "Eights!"

"Spot on. I've also managed to kit you out with some white flannels."

He wasn't at all sure he should play now with this sodding RAF officer in the side.

"You will play, of course, Joey?" Keith Fountain, the skipper of the club, joined their company.

"He'd love to, wouldn't you, Joey?" Tony placed the cricket boots on the bar stool in the corner.

"Do have another drink!" the skipper insisted.

"Try a glass of the President's champagne!" Charles tempted him from behind the bar.

Reminiscent of yesterday, bottles of the stuff began appearing on the scene. What a way to start a cricket match, thought Joey.

"Let me introduce you to the President, Joey," Keith offered, leading him outside onto the veranda where even more people were gathered now.

He was presented to a tall man with stooped shoulders, silver-grey hair, a face heavily lined and brown coloured eyes, the whites of which were bloodshot. Tweed-suited, he carried a gnarled and knotted walking stick in his right hand. A long-stemmed briar pipe hung from the corner of his thin-lipped mouth. His name was Henry Fitzgibbon, the president of Southbank Cricket Club. "Very good of you to play at such short notice, young feller," he spoke softly, shaking Joey rigorously by the hand.

"How do you do, sir!" Joey greeted him hospitably.

"I hear you've played some professional stuff?" He cupped the bowl of his pipe in the palm of his left hand; smoke curling from the corner of his mouth. Tired, brown eyes viewed Joey, his head tilted to one side.

"A little, yes," Joey confessed.

"We trust you'll be in good form today? I do like my side to win. See what you can do, eh? Got a drink? Lovely day for it? I must toddle off to see how the ladies are getting on with the lunches. Do have a nice day, young feller. Hope to see more of you in the future? Talk to you later, no doubt?"

"Goodbye, sir!" a chorus of voices respected the president's departure.

The skipper then introduced Joey to more Club members, one of these being a short, spectacled chap, his name, Martin Selby. Late thirties, he owned a mop of curly, fair hair. "P-p-pleased to meet you, Joey." He also had the misfortune of having an embarrassing speech impediment.

"Martin's a schoolmaster over at Glenton Park Preparatory School," the skipper informed Joey. "And the man standing next to him is Richard Benton who owns most of the surrounding land that you can see all around you. He's having enormous success with his riding school at the moment. Richard's one of our non playing members here at the cricket club. Golf is more his game."

A craggy-faced, trilby-hatted gent of around forty shook him by the hand. "Hello!" His greeting was most enthusiastic. "Any time you fancy going for a romp on the horses, let me know – I'll fix it up for you. Okay?"

"Yeah, okay." He couldn't picture himself sitting astride some wild stallion somehow though.

Next, a tall, lithe man, bald-headed except for a few greying temple hairs and who stood smoking a huge cigar. A broad smile spread across his face as they were introduced. "And this, Joey, is Squadron Leader

Cockshott of the Royal Air Force! An organisation with which you yourself are only too well familiar with"

Joey looked at the cigar-puffing officer standing in the open doorway.

"Charlie – I'd like you to meet a fellow Air Force service man – Corporal Joey Webster!"

Silence, as the officer eyed him up and down suspiciously. "I gather we're both playing in the same team together, Corporal?" the squadron leader finally addressed him.

"So I believe, sir!"

"Good show!"

Of all bloody people to bump into, thought Joey, cursing his luck at this cruel hand of fete being dealt to him in this manner.

"On a spot of leave, are we, Corporal?"

"Yes, sir! I have some time owing me." Another lie, but it sounded convincing enough.

Then Tony came bounding along the veranda carrying a sports holdall in one hand and waving a brand new cricket bat around in the other. "I see you two have met then?" He smiled at the two RAF personnel before dropping the bag at Joey's feet.

Cockshott looked down his nose at him and appeared to be irritated by this intrusion.

"Quiet, please!" Tony then commanded everybody's attention in a loud voice. "The Wevwent Mason is on his way up to the gwound. I think it is time that we all assembled out on the cwicket field to witness the cewemony."

On hearing this information, everyone began to move away from the pavilion.

"Someone better inform the President!" a concerned voice shouted.

Whatever the hell was happening, Joey felt grateful, as it had saved him from having to talk shop with old Cockshott, hadn't it? He was more than happy to tag on behind this sudden exodus toward the cricket pitch.

"Glorious day!" someone remarked as they strolled across the field together in the sunshine.

"I gather the President has been notified?" another person enquired anxiously.

"The ground's very hard!" someone else observed.

He went with the crowd like a lamb to slaughter. Heaven knows what they were all actually doing gathered out there in the middle of the bloody cricket field though!

Then Tony came to his rescue again with a quiet explanation in his ear. "This gwound blessing twadition goes way back. In fact, to the actual fowmation of the Southbank Club."

Over the heads of the people assembled at one end of the cricket square, Joey noticed a gent dressed in a long, black church cassock advancing toward them. Four young lads wearing white altar server's albs, followed close behind, one of whom was carrying a large, silver crucifix high above his head.

"They come fwom the chuwch acwoss the woad." Tony explained to him. "We always have a gwound blessing cewemony each season on this special day."

How many more surprises were there in store for him that day? Joey wondered to himself.

All was silent as the Reverend Mason came to a halt in front of the gathered congregation.

Joey stood at the back of the crowd straining with both ears in an attempt to listen to the blessing that this man of the cloth was now offering. It proved difficult with the noisy traffic outside the ground on the road nearby. He noticed the president of the Club standing with a group of fellow members close by. He also saw Charles Bellamy, serious-looking, watching the proceedings. The Bryant's were also present, their Rolls Royce car parked beneath a horse chestnut tree over in the shade behind which horses and riders romped about the field totally unperturbed by the goings on this side of the fence.

The Reverend Mason concluded the service by sprinkling water from a metal casket onto the cricket field. He then smiled and bade everyone farewell before walking off down the slope whence he came with his young assistants in pursuit.

"The vicar has very large ears, don't you think?" Joey overheard one of the ladies remarks as the gathering began to disperse.

"Didn't the young boys look sweet?" another commented.

He had heard of different cricket clubs and their customs through playing the game; but nothing to compare with this, that's for sure. It could be construed as an unfair advantage by the opposition that Southbank C.C. should have God influencing the outcome of the game in their favour perhaps?

He was about to enter the pavilion when Keith Fountain appeared at his side. "I've left some gear for you in the dressing room, Joey," he informed him.

"Cheers!" Joey thanked him as he caught sight of the drinks man standing outside on the veranda.

"So if you wouldn't mind getting changed – only there's a team photograph to be taken before the start of play. I'll go and round up the others."

Joey retrieved the cricket boots that Tony had left for him on the bar stool and went in search of the dressing room.

Chapter 8 Team Photograph

The dressing room was long and narrow with a rubber mat stretched down the centre of the floor. A window looked out onto the cricket field at the far end. Coat-hooks lined the walls with wooden benches beneath them on either side of the room. A large table stood in the middle on the floor.

He got changed into the clothes Keith had left for him and stood admiring himself in a mirror that hung from the wall just inside the door. The cricket shirt seemed a little on the tight side, but the trousers were a good fit. Boots, too. He wouldn't bother with the sweater on such a warm day. So, there he was, ready to do battle!

Charles Bellamy entered the room, accompanied by a tall, fair-haired man carry a large, leather cricket bag.

"I see they kitted you out all right then, Joey?" Charles face was becoming redder and redder as the day wore on.

"Yeah, they did me proud." Joey proceeded to hang the clothes he had changed out of onto a vacant hook.

"This is Corporal Joey Webster of the Royal Air Force, Ronnie. Prior to that he was a professional cricketer on the Middlesex ground staff."

"Really – how interesting." The new acquaintance dropped his bag to the floor with a heavy thud and offered Joey his hand.

"I'd like you to meet Ronnie Ainsworth, Joey - skipper of the President's side today. You've no doubt heard him commentating the Test Matches for the BBC on the radio?"

Of course he had – he knew he'd heard that voice somewhere before.

"Nice to meet you, Joey." The voice shook him cordially by the hand.

"I'll leave you two to get on with it then." Charles departed with a smile.

"How did you manage to be playing for the President's team today, Joey?" the refined speaking BBC man enquired in a friendly manner.

Joey kicked his shoes under the bench. "Purely by chance really. I happened to meet up with some of the Southbank members at Lord's yesterday."

"I see."

The man completed his change of dress and stood with his foot resting on the bench as he tied the long, white lace of his cricket boot. "How long were you up at Lord's then, Joey?"

"In all – three seasons."

"Will you be going back there at all?"

Joey looked with interest at this likeable, well-educated gentleman with the clear, blue eyes, straight nose and firm jaw. "I hardly think so – not now."

The commentator then produced a cricket blazer from out of his bag. Striped and rainbow-coloured, Jacob from the Old Testament would undoubtedly have been proud to wear it. "Do you think the camera will take kindly to it, Joey?" The quip brought a cheeky smile to his face.

Joey stared with amusement at both man and blazer.

"Shall we go and put it to the test?"

On the field outside, the president's team had arranged themselves on a couple of long benches directly in front of the pavilion to have their photographs taken. An elderly gent, tall, with a stooped body, hovered patiently over proceedings after having designated positions for everyone to take up.

"Hurry along, you two!" the president chastised his skipper and Joey in good humour as they made their way down onto the grass to join the group.

"Sorry I'm a little late, sir!" Ronnie Ainsworth offered his apologies. "Got rather held up in the traffic. You know how it is?"

The president rose to his feet and shook his hand. "How are you, dear boy?"

"I'm fine, thank you. Glorious day for the match, sir?"

Joey was ushered to the back of the group by the photographer, while the BBC man sat down next to the president in the front. "Are all of your team present now, Mr. Fitzgibbon?" A cigarette hung from the corner of the photographer's yellow-stained mouth.

"Yes, all here thank you, Mr. Potts!" The president removed his pipe from his mouth to take up a pose for the long awaited team picture.

Mr. Potts gave a final glance at the assembled players before hiding himself behind his camera, which was positioned on a tripod on the grass. "Look this way, please, gentlemen!"

The usual comments of, "Cheese!" reserved for occasions such as these were uttered by various individuals, followed by sniggers before 'click' of the camera.

Joey glanced to his immediate left to discover old Cockshott standing beside him with an expression on his dark-skinned face that for all the world might have given one the impression he could have been a commanding officer in charge of a squadron of fighter pilots just returned from a successful bombing mission. And here was Joey having his photograph taken with them. If this didn't beat all, he thought with amusement, looking quickly back at the camera and wondering to himself what on earth sergeant Cummins would make of it all.

Another 'click' and, "Thank you, gentlemen!" from old Potts, before lighting himself a fresh cigarette.

Joey had turned to make his way back to the pavilion when the squadron leader confronted him. "Managed to get yourself kitted out all right, I see, Corporal?"

He stopped momentarily in his tracks, hoping someone would come to his rescue; but no one was at hand at that precise moment.

"Yes, sir!" He supposed it was inevitable that they should meet again sometime or other?

"Tell me; are you a bat or bowler, Webster?"

"All-rounder, sir!"

Joey observed some horses jauntily galloping about in the field behind the officer. It made him feel quite envious of their freedom and he suddenly wished he could change places with them.

"Are we now?" The officer's remark sounded patronising. "Do you come from this part of the world, Webster?"

"I'm from Wufton, sir!"

"Ah! Just up the road. On leave for long, are we?"

"Just a fortnight, sir! Then I'm due for my demob."

They reached the pavilion steps.

"Not signing on for another spell with us then, Corporal?" the officer persisted with his damned questioning, lighting himself another cigar, his rosy cheeks working hard to get it going.

"Most definitely not, sir!" Joey was becoming more and more annoyed with this man's constant prying into his affairs, making him feel extremely uncomfortable, even inferior really. He suddenly wanted to be on the cricket field where he would bloody well show them all that out there having a superior rank meant sod all.

"By the way, Corporal – where are you stationed?"

At long last, the sixty four thousand dollar question! Joey faked a cough, looked away from him, and noticed the president advancing toward them. Saved by the bell again!

"Be a good sport and find Richard Benson for me, would you, Squadron Leader?" he asked the officer politely. "Only I'm not at all sure if he has guests staying for lunch or not. Could you possibly find out, there's a good chap? Many thanks."

"Certainly, Henry." Cockshott shot off in pursuit of the farmer.

"Getting on all right, are we, young man?" The president sounded genuinely concerned for Joey's welfare.

"I'm fine, thank you, sir!" Joey felt grateful to the old boy for having come along to his rescue when he did.

"Ol' Potts will be through in a minute. Then the game can get under way." He paused for a moment, seemingly to gather his thoughts. "Well, do have a nice day then, young man. Yes, I'll see you later..."

He walked slowly away.

Then Tony came bounding up the steps, smiling, and looking full of energy. "Clothes the wight size, Joey?"

Joey thrust his hands deep inside his trouser pockets, the right one having a large hole, he discovered.

"By the way – the Pwesident's side is fielding! The captains have just tossed – Keith called cowect and has decided to bat."

"I see."

"You've met the captain, Wonnie, haven't you?"

"Yes, in the dressing room earlier."

"He'll soon put you wight."

Tony then disappeared inside the pavilion to leave Joey standing on his own again and very vulnerable once more to further advances that officer Cockshott might make toward him. It wasn't long either before he appeared back on the scene, accompanied by Richard Benton and another gent who was small and plump with a ruddy complexion and silver-grey hair.

"I better go have a word with Henry," the farmer muttered, passing Joey by and giving him a friendly smile.

"When's this bloody cricket match supposed to start then?" shouted the red-faced man standing with Cockshott, a drink in his hand and swaying on his feet.

"Shouldn't be too long now, Stuart." The squadron leader looked a little embarrassed at this sudden outburst from his colleague as he caught Joey's eye. "Stuart, I'd like you to meet Corporal Webster who is playing in the President's side today."

Glassy-blue eyes focused on Joey, looking him up and down. "Hello, young man." It was more of a mumble than an actual greeting. The warm, pleasant smile that accompanied it was real enough though.

"This is Stuart Henderson, Corporal," Cockshott introduced the man to him. "Stuart used to captain the Club here at one time."

With feet planted firmly, a drink in his hand, this one-time skipper stood gazing at Joey through squinting eyes. "Corporal, eh?" His voice had a somewhat gruff resonance to it. "Well, we can't keep calling you bloody Corporal now, can we? What's your real name, boy?"

Instantly, Joey knew he would like him. He didn't really know why, but could sense that here was a true man of the world. A no-nonsense man, calling a spade a spade and standing for no bull shit! In fact, a hardworking, hard drinking man.

"It's Joey," he informed him proudly.

"Joey, eh? Yes, I like it. Well, Joey – would you like to join me in a drink?"

"Should I – just before the game?"

"Of course you should. How about you, Squadron Leader?"

Cockshott puffed away at his cigar. "Yes, I'd love to, Stuart."

Joey accompanied both men in the direction of the serving hatch of the bar.

"Gangway, please!" Stuart shouted for the benefit of the crowd who were clustered at the far end of the veranda as he pushed his way through them.

"Stuart, darling!" Tony's wife, sipping champagne, greeted the jovial man with a smile.

"Carol – how nice to see you." He kissed her on the cheek and pinched her rather shapely bottom.

"And how is the Squadron Leader keeping?" A tall man with a thin pencil-line moustache made this enquiry. "Not playing today, are we?"

"But of course, Reggie – I never miss this match, ol' boy."

"If I may please have your attention. . !" Stuart then addressed everyone, raising his hands above his head. "Today is my twenty-fifth wedding anniversary and I would like you all to join me in a drink to celebrate this memorable and happy occasion."

For a moment there was a hushed silence. Then: "Hurrah! Good old Stuart!" from everybody.

"Right, open the bubbly then, please, Charles!"

Charles Bellamy began to noisily uncork the champagne bottles reserved for this event. Glasses were then filled to overflowing and toasts offered for Stuart and his noticeably absent wife.

At five minutes past twelve precisely the cricket match finally got under way; but only then after everyone present had sampled the champagne that was on offer.

Chapter 9 The Cricket Match

The BBC man led the president's side out onto the cricket field. The white-coated umpires had taken up their respective positions either end of the cricket square and stood waiting for the players to join them.

Joey couldn't remember having seen these two characters until now, which, he supposed was only typical where umpires of a cricket match were concerned, their presence only actually being felt when a decision of some kind needed making. Only then did any of the players – or spectators for that matter – seemed aware of their existence. Leastways, that was what he thought, or indeed, had experienced many times himself in the past. Today, however, possibly because he was a complete stranger to the two sides, not to mention the class difference with them also, he felt the need to strike up a conversation with the umpire standing at the bottom end while the BBC man began his field positioning for the opening bowler.

"Nice day!" Joey remarked.

"It most certainly is, young fellow." He was a small man, round-faced with a pointed nose and sporting a white-flecked, nanny-goat beard. "Aren't you the RAF boy?"

"That's me, yeah."

"I hear you spent some time at Lord's?"

"That's right."

"What do you think of our Club then?"

"It seems very nice."

"Yes, it's not bad here. One or two odd types – but pay them no heed. You'll be all right."

"I'm sure I will."

Joey certainly felt very happy with the warm sun on his back and with the picturesque scene before him. The umpire smiled at him. He appreciated his few words of kindness and obvious concern for his welfare in mixing with this particular crowd. He was convinced though that any inhibitions he may have been experiencing with their actual acceptance of him would very soon disappear once the game commenced. Any barrier between him and these toffs would then ultimately be lifted. For then he would be participating in something where one's financial status meant bugger all, and any irritations caused by this fact for him like what particular type school he went to or the size of house he owned or the model of car he drove were of no real importance out there on the cricket field.

He was therefore looking forward to the actual game very much indeed, not just because he wanted to do well or to show this lot how good he was at the sport, but also to feel he could be accepted by them, despite having none of their material advantages in life.

"Would you like to take first slip, please, Joey?" the BBC man designated him his fielding position.

He walked across the closely mown, green sward of the cricket square to take up his post beside a rather large, pot-bellied, red-gloved wicket keeper.

"Second slip, please, Alan!"

The squadron leader was at the receiving end of an order for a change as he made his way over to join Joey.

If this didn't beat everything! thought Joey with a wry smile on his face. Here he was, absent without leave from his unit and standing right next to a bloody RAF squadron leader as they were about to participate in a village cricket match together. It really was quite unbelievable.

"Leave it to the good old Air Force to guard this area of hostilities, eh, Corporal?" the officer remarked in all seriousness, taking up his position next to Joey.

"Yes, sir!" Although agreeing with his statement, Joey was finding it hard not to take the rise out of the silly old fool.

"We will let nothing – absolutely nothing through our line of defence here, eh, Corporal?"

"Absolutely not, sir!"

The opening Southbank batsman asked for his guard from the umpire with a two-fingered gesture that anyone not familiar with the game of cricket might interpret as meaning something totally different and be extremely offended by it.

"That is middle an' leg, sir!" The umpire, wearing dark sunglasses, acknowledged the players request. Then, unfolding a shooting stick that hung from his arm placed it firmly in the ground behind him and sat down upon its leather-bound seat. After glancing around the field to ensure everything was now in order for commencement of the game, he folded his arms and uttered in a voice full of authority: "PLAY!"

A young, fair-haired, broad-shouldered lad came pounding in on a long run to bowl the first delivery of the match. And what a peach of a ball it was. Perfect length, it drew the batsman forward, the cherry-red ball moving away from him late and finding the outside edge of his white-bladed bat as it swiftly sped off in the direction of slips where it hit old Cockshott hard on the toe of his right boot.

The squadron leader let out a suppressed yelp as the ball carried off to the boundary for four runs. "Chrisake!" he cried between clenched teeth, hopping about the field on one leg. "That's damned unfriendly, wouldn't you say, ol' sport?"

Joey found it hard not to burst out laughing at the incident as the officer began frantically exercising his injured toe back to life, this resulting in some considerable time being lost before the game was allowed to continue.

About forty-five minutes into proceedings, the umpire with whom Joey had conversed with earlier had to leave the field of play suffering from sunstroke.

"I see Bertie's up to his old tricks again?" The BBC man appeared to be somewhat agitated with the umpire's decision to abandon the players in this fashion.

"Yes, time for his pre-lunch drink as usual" Cockshott implied sarcastically.

"Old Bertie's perfectly all right really," the wicket keeper informed Joey while they waited for a replacement umpire to come onto the field. "He always pulls a fast one like this to enable him time for a quiet Guinness or two before the luncheon interval."

This tit-bit of information didn't surprise Joey in the least. He was convinced that anything could happen with this lot.

Fifteen minutes later the umpires removed the bails from the stumps and they all strolled off the field for lunch themselves. It had been the shortest pre-luncheon cricket session Joey had ever experienced. The opposing team's score stood at sixty-five runs for the loss of no wickets, with their opening bat having made thirty-three and his partner twenty two respectively. There were ten extras.

They entered the pavilion amid applause from various club members and the general spectators.

Chapter 10 President's Lunch

The president's lunch that followed proved to be quite an affair. Before sitting down to it they all stood about in groups drinking and talking about the morning's cricket. The majority of players wore blazers; Ronnie Ainsworth's being the most colourful of these as he chatted with friends up at the bar.

"How's the commentating going these days, Wonnie?" Tony sounded genuinely interested to hear how the BBC man was progressing in his chosen profession with the corporation.

"Fine, thank you, Tony," he replied, standing very erect, smoking a cigarette, drinking a glass of sherry, his sharp, blue eyes admiring the beauty of the questionnaire's wife, who, sipping her gin and tonic, stood opposite.

"Is your wife coming along later?" Carol's eyes looked admiringly into those of the celebrity's.

"She said she would, yes."

Joey stood quietly on his own sipping a beer, feeling rather left out of things and secretly wishing that Lesley were there to talk to and keep him company. He glanced out the open window of the pavilion, the hum of conversation from everyone gathered inside droning in his ears, while outside the sun continued to shine down on a bright, tranquil, summer scene.

Like a bad penny, old Cockshott suddenly appeared at his side again to annoy him further with his inquisitive third degree questioning. "What is it you actually do in the RAF, Corporal – your trade?"

Joey felt annoyed at himself for not having noticed the officer creeping up on him from behind in this fashion to seek out his company. "I'm an Officers Mess steward, sir!"

"Really?"

He's bound to bloody well ask where I'm stationed now, thought Joey as he watched him light up a fresh cigar; but, as luck would have it, the president appeared on the scene to save his bacon.

"If you wouldn't mind, gentlemen!" he addressed them both, placing a friendly hand on Cockshott's shoulder. "Time for lunch!"

The bell had saved him again.

"I'll leave you to it then, Webster." Cockshott excused himself to go and sit with Richard Benton at the meal table.

Joey felt relieved knowing he wouldn't be sitting next to the squadron leader during lunch as he found himself a space at the far end of the table near to the bar on the right, the pavilion door just behind him wide open on this hot summer afternoon.

The president sat at the head of the table between the two respective captains. When everyone was all sitting down, he rose to his feet and called for silence by banging on the table with a small wooden mallet. In the quietness that followed, he bowed his head to offer grace.

"For what we are about to receive, may the Lord make us truly thankful!" His spoken words were uttered with the utmost sincerity.

Mumblings of: "Amen!" came from the lips of the assembled, followed immediately by excited chatter.

"Would you mind passing the potatoes down, ol' boy?" This request came from one obviously hungry young cricketer close by as the sounds of knives and forks in action, intermingled with conversation then filled the pavilion as everyone set about devouring the food before them.

"Settled in all right, have we, young man?" Joey found himself on the same table as the enquiring sunstroke-suffering umpire.

He swallowed a portion of juicy tomato with a slice of tasty ham. "Yeah, fine thanks. How are you now – have you recovered?"

"I'm much better, thank you, lad. I'll be as right as rain after lunch. A slight touch of the sun, that's all. Nothing to worry about."

The man drank his Guinness, belched and stroked the end of his beard with his long fingers. "Bet they don't look after you at Lord's like this, eh?"

Joey made no reply to his statement, busy enjoying his food. He noticed Tony looking at him from the opposite side of the table.

"Did you make out all wight with old Cockshott then, Joey?"

"Not so bad." He washed some food down with a glass of refreshing cool ale as he sucked at a piece of meat that had got lodged between his teeth.

Tony munched his lettuce. "He's not a bad chap weally, I suppose."

"Damned ruddy lazy, if you ask me," the umpire remarked.

"That's sewvice life fowa you." Tony persevered with the lettuce. "Would you agwee, Joey?"

"I think it can make you lazy, yes." In his opinion, he honestly believed it to be true, especially if you happened to be a commissioned officer.

Ice-cream and fruit was then served to them by two of the smiling ladies he had seen earlier in the Tea Hut, followed by cheese and biscuits, coffee, then port and sherry that they poured for themselves from impressive looking twin-glass decanters that made their way slowly round the table.

The president rose to his feet. "You may now smoke if you wish, ladies and gentlemen!" he announced in a clear, distinctive voice before sitting down again.

Deep sighs of appreciation from the smoking clientele gathered greeted this statement.

"Fancy one of these, young man?" The umpire offered Joey a large cigar.

"Don't mind if I do," Joey thanked him, and after lighting it up, sat back in his chair to sample a large glass of port as he thoroughly enjoyed this part of the proceedings, finishing things off as far as he was concerned in right bloody style.

The president then rose again and proceeded to bang the table with his mallet to gain everybody's attention. "Ladies and gentlemen! It is so nice to see you all gathered here today for this annual cricket match. And on such a glorious day as well. I'm very glad you could all make it, and I sincerely hope you enjoy yourselves." He paused to look down at some notes he had prepared for the occasion. Clearing his throat, he continued: "I'll start by giving thanks to Ronnie for taking on board the very hazardous task of skippering my side this year."

"Hear! Hear!" someone agreed wholeheartedly.

The president continued with his amusing speech, going on to talk about the general history of the Southbank Cricket Club while cracking jokes in between that everyone politely laughed at. He concluded finally by saying: "Of course, as we are all only too fully aware, the game wouldn't be possible without the vast amount of behind the scene work that is carried out by a certain few, some of whom I would now like to mention, if I may. Yes. . ." Another glance at his notes was again necessary at this point. "To begin with I would like to thank our dear old friend Ben Tunney, who, as always has been responsible in organising the splendid lunches that we have all just been privileged enough to have eaten. On behalf of everyone present, Ben, we thank you very much – we're most grateful to you."

A thunderous round of applause greeted a certain gentleman seated at a table by the open window of the pavilion; all of the women-folk present also occupying this table. Ben Tunney rose to his feet to acknowledge this ovation, a broad smile spread across his rather red face. After taking a quick bow, he then sat down again, Tony's wife, to the left of him, whispering something in his ear that made him chuckle with glee.

"Could we also please show our appreciation for the marvellous ladies present here and for their help today? Thank you very much, ladies!"

More applause, the women-folk all-beaming with smiles, some of them even blushing at suddenly becoming the centre of attraction.

"Yes. . ." The president glanced at his notes one final time. "I would also like to sincerely thank Charles for running the bar on such a busy day that we all know this to be. Many thank, Charles!"

"Well done, Charles!" voices repeated the president's praises for the man in question.

The president cracked a final joke that everyone seemed to find very amusing, and then finished his speech by saying: "All that remains now is to hope the game that follows will be as enjoyable as this delicious luncheon has been and I'm sure everyone will be more than satisfied. I will now pass you over into the capable hands of my captain, who, I'm sure needs no introduction really. Thanks very much for coming today and God bless you all."

Joey joined with the rest in applauding this very fine speech, and then took the liberty of helping himself to another glass of port from the passing decanter.

Now it was time for Ronnie Ainsworth to deliver his speech. "Ladies and gentlemen!" he began in confident mood. "I must say how thrilled I am to be here to captain dear Henry's side today. Indeed, I class it as an honour, I assure you. . ."

Talking for about five minutes or so about the game of cricket, about the Club, Ronnie Ainsworth then closed his narration by asking everyone present to be upstanding in offering a toast to their president.

They all rose to the occasion to honour their host.

"The President!" they chanted as they downed their ports and sherries.

Fifteen minutes later the cricket match was allowed to resume once more, the actual time of day now being two-thirty precisely, the longest cricket luncheon interval Joey had ever experienced in his life.

At ten minutes to four that afternoon, Keith Fountain declared the Southbank innings closed with their score at 185 for the loss of

6 wickets, the opening batsman having contributed a very fine 90 out of this total before being adjudged out L.B.W. Joey was given a few overs to bowl toward the finish and managed to bag himself a couple of wickets in the process which pleased him immensely. However, conditions seemed to favour the batsmen generally, and what with the short boundary, plenty of fours and sixes were hit during the course of play.

Tea was then taken, during which time the groundsman brushed, rolled and remarked the wicket.

"Would you like to open the innings for us, Joey?" Ronnie Ainsworth, lighting his cigarette, asked him during the interval.

"Yeah, if you want." Joey felt honoured at being asked to shoulder this responsibility.

"You can use my bat if you wish, Joey?" This offer came from Tony who was seated opposite.

"The Squadron Leader can partner you, I think." The BBC man scribbled his batting order on a piece of paper. "Will that suit you all right, Alan?"

Cockshott's face appeared from behind a cream cake. "It certainly will, ol' boy. I rather fancy myself out there today." He looked over at Joey, a dollop of cream adorning his top lip. "We'll bloody well show 'em, Corporal, won't we? We'll make sure our side gets off to a flying start, eh? What do you say?"

If the old boy's batting was anything like his fielding, they wouldn't, that's for sure, Joey thought as he finished drinking his cup of tea.

However, the squadron leader proved to be quite a competent batsman, scoring 15 of the first 25 runs that the pair of them added in the twenty minutes play immediately following the tea interval. Joey liked very much the way the old chap ran between the wickets, his actual calling of a run sound and well thought out so that after a while batting together they each trusted the others judgement implicitly.

And now, with the sun on his back and with his eye seeing the ball well, Joey began to set about attacking the Southbank bowling. Now, he was doing what he knew best, and was in his glory as he executed shots masterfully, gracefully, the runs clicking up on the scoreboard with regularity as he cut, drove, glanced, hooked, deflected, swept, punched the ball to all four corners of the ground, the ball a red blur as it sped across the turf in the brilliant sunshine. Finally, with twenty minutes left remaining to play and their side needing just 38 runs to win, he was brilliantly caught out on the boundary for 110. A very memorable afternoon indeed for him.

He felt extremely pleased with himself as he strode off the field and into the pavilion after his dismissal as both players and spectators alike gave him a standing ovation for his very fine performance.

"Well played, sir!" Charles Bellamy congratulated him afterwards inside the dressing room, thrusting a pint of beer into his perspiring hand as a reward for his outstanding effort.

"Just what I need, thanks!" Joey gasped, gulping it down quickly.

Tony appeared in the doorway. "Absolutely splendid knock, Joey!" He was smiling profusely as he complimented him excitedly. "My bat all wight, was it?"

"Yeah, great." Joey wiped his forehead with the back of his hand.

Charles took the empty beer mug from him. "There's a Miss Williams asking for you outside, Joey."

"Thanks."

"She arrived about half hour ago. I found a seat for her by the serving hatch. I'll tell her you'll be out shortly, shall I?"

"Fine. Thanks for your beer, by the way."

"The pleasure's all mine. Very seldom have I seen an innings of such class and distinction as was yours today, young man. Well done!"

Applause from outside, and the voice of someone shouting: "Run up! Run up!" could be heard coming from beneath the dressing room window. Wondering how the game was progressing, and looking forward very much to seeing Lesley again, he took some money from his other trousers, then left to find Lesley. He would change into his other clothes later after a hot shower.

He found her sitting outside at the end of the veranda. Behind her on the grass verge the scoreboard showed the president's side within twenty runs of victory. It looked like being a close thing as there were only ten minutes of actual playing time remaining before the close of play.

"Hello!" He approached Lesley with a welcoming smile.

She looked up, her attractive face breaking into her dimpled smile, indicating she was more than pleased to see him. Her hair had been newly groomed and looked extremely becoming. "Hello!" she spoke to him softly. "I've been told you have done exceptionally well today?"

He positioned himself behind her seat and leant his back against the timbered wall of the pavilion to view the closing stages of the game. "Yeah, you could say that." He felt like the cat that got the cream.

She offered him a cigarette.

"Thanks – I could certainly do with one."

"Oh, good shot, sir!" Cockshott, perched on a stool behind them in the bar shouted through the open window to congratulate the batsman out at the wicket for striking a colossal six that sent the ball clear over the top of the hedge at the far end of the ground and into the road outside, everyone wildly applauding this tremendous achievement with rapturous enthusiasm.

"By the way, Corporal – well played – splendid knock of yours!" The squadron leader appeared to be extremely pleased with Joey's performance. Not that the officer had done too badly himself, having scored 35 out of their opening partnership of 58 together before being given out L.B.W.

At the moment their side needed just 10 for victory with just five minutes left to play. Could they possibly do it?

They did – off the final delivery of the day with another mighty six that went sailing right over the top of the pavilion roof, coming to rest in Richard Benton's field beyond.

The players and officials trooped off the field after a very exciting game amid wild applause from everyone.

"What a wonderful finish to the contest." Lesley couldn't hide her enjoyment at being a witness to this final climatic ending to the cricketing contest.

"Marvellous! Truly marvellous!" an exuberant Joey exclaimed, feeling pleased with their side's winning result, and even more so with his own personal contribution. "Let's have a drink to celebrate, shall we?"

Chapter 11 Fire!

They stood around on the veranda enjoying a drink with groups of others doing likewise, some of the players, like him, still dressed in their cricketing attire. The sun, which had been so kind to them all day, began sinking slowly down the sky behind the pavilion, casting shadows of the scene onto the emerald-green grass of the cricket field.

"And where on earth did you vanish to last night, may I ask?" Joey questioned his charming companion.

Lesley sipped her drink slowly. "The Doctor wanted me to go with him in case his wife needed me for anything." Her sweet explanation sounded rather too good to be true really.

"And did she – want for anything, I mean?"

"No – she remained sound asleep all evening."

An awkward silence followed.

"There's no need to explain if you don't want. . ."

Their eyes met and they smiled at each other.

"I suppose you've guessed what happened anyway?"

"I think I have, yes."

"What is your deduction then, Mr. Holmes?"

He sampled a measure of his cool beer. "Well, what I think took place is this," he began slowly. "The real reason why the Doctor wanted you to accompany him on a visit to Harley Street was so that he could have the evening free in which to meet jolly ol' Tony's wife at a secret rendezvous somewhere – correct?"

"Now that you mention it he did say he had some business to attend to the other side of London, yes. He could have arranged a meeting there with Carol I suppose."

"Did you have any callers at Harley Street after he dropped you off?" Joey felt certain that that was where Tony was headed for after leaving the party last night.

"Yes – Tony, as a matter of fact."

"Uh – I thought as much."

"Which proves that you're getting just as observant as I am?"

"Yeah – two of a kind, ain't we?"

The president then joined their company, leaning on his cane and puffing his pipe. "Ah! Mi..shh William..shh," he spoke softly, his brown eyes looking tired and bloodshot, his speech noticeably affected by his over indulgence of alcohol. "Ju..shh to congratulate your good cricketing friend Shh..ergeant Web..shh..ter here on shh..uch a wonderful inning..shh thi..shh afternoon." He swayed on his feet, his thin, supportive cane bending dangerously beneath his weight.

"Thank you very much, sir!" Joey felt highly honoured at this sudden promotion in rank bestowed upon him by the old fellow.

The president removed the pipe from his mouth. "It ha..shh been an ab..shh..olute plea..shh..ure having you in my team, young man." His ramblings were becoming more and more incoherent. "Y-you mu..shh come and play for me again shh..umtime."

With this departing speech, he moved away; but only after some difficulty, his cane having become wedged between the wooden boards of the veranda. After some furious tugging he managed to free it, his efforts throwing him off balance, making him stumble as he set off to seek fresh company.

"A case of having too much to drink I would say, wouldn't you?" Lesley commented with a chuckle.

"Most definitely," Joey agreed with wry amusement. "No reason why we shouldn't partake in another though, is it?"

With dusk now descending, other cars, their headlights blazing, kept swinging into the ground from off the road down by the Club's entrance, search lighting their way up to the pavilion. Greetings of: "Hello! George!" "How are you, darling?" "Nice to see you, dear fellow!" came from different acquaintances as the owners and passengers of these vehicles entered the pavilion. Among these new arrivals were the Bryant's, who, shortly after the game finished, had slipped away in their Rolls, only to return again now with a change of clothing to participate in some evening drinking.

"I wonder how old moneybags there made his fortune." Joey watched Bryant ordering a round of drinks up at the bar.

"Dealing in property, that's where." Lesley was quick to inform him of this knowledge.

"And Tony – what does he do?"

Lesley leant back on the wall of the pavilion. "Motor industry," she enlightened him, gazing up into Joey's eyes.

He returned her gaze, her blue eyes distracting him from pursuing the subject further, making him realize that perhaps he should be paying her a little more attention.

A silence followed. Then, as if it was a perfectly natural thing for them both to do, they stood and held hands together.

"Thank you, Joey."

"For what?"

"For inviting me along today."

After a moment, he said: "The pleasure's all mine, I can assure you."

He felt her hand tighten in his.

"Tell me, Lesley – do you manage to get out on occasions like this?" He was interested to know whether she made a habit of socialising with these particular people to see just what kind of opposition he was up against.

She gave his question some considerable thought, before answering: "Yes, quite a lot really, I suppose."

"I see." His reply sounded rather despondent.

But then she smiled at him and added kindly, purely for his benefit, he thought: "But not always with the company I would prefer, Joey."

Charles Bellamy appeared inside the frame of the serving hatch. "I see you are in the best of company, Miss Williams?" He looked down at them in the prevailing darkness outside with a broad smile on his face.

"I most certainly am, Mr. Bellamy, aren't I?" Lesley chuckled.

"Only the very best!" Joey was in full agreement with the gent's statement as he laughed at the private joke that he and his attractive escort were sharing.

"I better leave you to it then, eh?" quipped Charles as he disappeared back in behind the bar.

"Nice geezer?"

"Yes, the perfect gentleman."

They each lit a cigarette before continuing with their drinking, with their conversation.

Then, quite suddenly and without any warning, it happened.

"Fire!" a woman's voice screamed from inside the building. "The pavilion's on fire..!"

"My God! Get the ladies outside, quick!" a concerned man's voice shouted with alarm.

Within seconds, everyone was safely evacuated from the pavilion. And within seconds also, flames rose to engulf the whole of the inside of the building. Charles Bellamy managed to save a few of the Club's photographs, snatching them off the walls as he charged out from the blazing inferno before the whole place went up like matchwood.

The entire gathering, who, only a few minutes earlier had been standing inside the pavilion socialising, were now all assembled outside on the cricket field witnessing the destruction of their beloved Club House in front of their very eyes, their faces wearing horrorstricken expressions as the pavilion burned brightly away in the darkness of the night.

Joey stood beside Lesley with her hand anxiously grasping his as they both watched this terrifying spectacle in mournful silence, hardly able to believe what they were witnessing.

"I-I wonder how it started..?" a woman's voice to their left enquired, breaking the silence that had momentarily befell all onlookers.

"Yes, I wonder..?" questioned a man's voice suspiciously.

"It's a catastrophe!" Charles Bellamy stood sobbing in front of them cradling a pile of framed pictures lovingly in his arms with tears running down his crimson cheeks. What a tragic blow this was for him. He looked completely crushed by it all.

A few minutes later a fire engine with siren wailing came racing along the road outside, and then, swinging in to the cricket ground, sped towards the pavilion. Water hydrants were very quickly located, the hoses connected to them, as firemen raced about in all directions.

It took an hour to eventually put out the fire. Questions from the fire chief then followed. Apparently, it had begun in the president's dressing room, probably from a lighted cigarette.

It was with sudden horror that Joey then realized he had left some money in the back pocket of his other trousers in there. "My God!" It was a gasp of sheer exasperation on his part, for he could ill afford the loss of any of this cash.

"What's the matter, Joey?" Lesley asked with alarm.

"My trousers! They were inside the dressing room."

"Oh..!"

From the cluster of people in front of them, he noticed the president leaning wearily on his cane with a worn, haggard look on his lined face as he watched the firemen finally complete their hazardous work. Standing by him, the farmer, Richard Benton, his long legs astride, his muscular arms folded across his barrel-shaped chest seemed visibly shaken by what he saw. Then the squadron leader, his usual carefree expression noticeably absent from his countenance because of these present events, viewed the scene in disbelief. Alongside him, the ruddy-faced Stuart Henderson, a glass clutched in his hand and obviously endeavouring to cheer everyone up, exclaimed: "Never mind! The ol' place was getting a bit past it! We'll just have to build a new one now, won't we? I move that we all pop across the Noke to discuss future plans over a drink, wot?"

"An admirable idea, if I may say so, Stuart" The president had no hesitation in agreeing with this suggestion, no doubt wanting to leave the scene of such devastation to their beloved cricket pavilion.

They all began making their way across the field and out through a small gate in the hedge behind the sight screens to enter the quaint old pub with its sign THE NOKE hanging from its red-bricked wall outside.

Joey and Lesley both remained close together, and, after getting themselves a drink from the bar, which Lesley paid for now that he had no immediate money to hand, they went outside to sit on a bench.

They sat in silence for some moments with their thoughts pondering on the burning down of the cricket pavilion. The tragedy had ruined what had been up until then a wonderful day for everyone. Luckily though, no one had sustained any injury from the occurrence.

"It's such a terrible shame." Lesley moved closer to him.

"Yeah, a real shame." Joey couldn't hide his sadness. "I just feel so sorry for all of them. The President – everybody..."

"I know – it's such a pity." She reached out for his hand. "There's not much we can do about unfortunately, is there?"

He gazed into her sympathetic eyes. "No, not really."

They sat quietly holding hands and watched the traffic drive by on the road in front of them.

Lesley then surprised him a little by saying: "Would you like to come back to Harley Street for a coffee before returning to your hotel, Joey?"

He felt excited at this suggestion. Wondering what episode of his life was about to unfold, he enquired rather tentatively: "But what about the Doctor?"

"What about him?"

"Won't he mind?"

"I shouldn't think so – he's away with his wife at their place in the country. They go there most week-ends in the summer."

"Do they?"

He got to his feet. "I think it's an excellent idea, Lesley," he said to her quietly. "I'll just return our glasses and say cheerio to everyone first though."

He found Tony standing up at the bar with numerous other Southbank members. "I've got to be going now." He had grown quite fond of this likeable character. "I'll pop the cricket flannels back to you as soon as possible."

"All wight, ol' chap! Pity about what happened, eh?"

"Yeah, a great pity."

Keith Fountain caught his eye. "Well played, Joey. That was a brilliant knock of yours. Don't lose touch now..?"

"Ye..shh, do come and play for ushh again, won't you, young man?" the president added, slumped in a chair by the window, the long, eventful day obviously proving too much for the old boy.

"Well, thank you very much for the game." He noticed Charles Bellamy also slumped in a chair beside the president.

The well-mannered gent nodded his head in Joey's direction, and, from the vague look on his tired face, seemed quite oblivious to the goings on around him. "Catastrophe! An absolute bloody catastrophe," he was murmuring to himself.

With these sad mutterings, Joey walked slowly out of the bar to rejoin Lesley.

Chapter 12 Harley Street

They journeyed back to Harley Street on the tube train, with Joey feeling somewhat conspicuous dressed as he was in his cricket flannels; but after alighting from the carriage at Baker Street it didn't seem quite so bad once they began walking the short distance from the station to the doctor's residence.

"You go on up to my room – I'll make the coffee," Lesley said to him in the hallway after opening a large door at the top of some marble steps outside.

Joey stood inside the high-ceiling house observing old and cracked oil paintings that hung from clean distempered walls with a long mirror and a narrow table on the left close to the entrance.

"I'm the second door on the right." She pointed up the stairs. "I shan't be long. Turn on the light by the wall as you enter."

"Thanks." He was feeling a little nervous as he began slowly climbing the thick-carpeted stairway that had more paintings lining the walls on the way up.

"Make yourself at home, won't you. . ?"

He located her room successfully, pushed open the door, searched for the light switch. A large lamp-shaded light lit up a narrow room in front of a tall window that looked out onto the street and other residences opposite. A white lace curtain moved silently to and fro in the calm breeze blowing through the open window. He moved toward a low sofa on the left by the wall, a bookcase with numerous books on display next to it. A dressing- table with a chair in front was positioned the other side near to the window. Joey sat himself on the sofa, a coffee table close by. He couldn't help but notice the bed on the far side of the room against the wall, a green bedspread draped neatly over it.

Lesley entered, carrying a tray. "Here we are." She placed it on the table beside him. "Do you take sugar?"

He sat nervously twiddling his thumbs. "Please, two."

She poured them a coffee, glancing up at him in the process. "Don't look so worried, Joey. Here – drink this up like a good boy and then you can go."

Her remark surprised him a little. After all, he didn't really want to return to his hotel just yet.

"I hope the coffee's to your liking?"

He sipped it slowly. "Yes, it's very nice, thanks." He couldn't remember having been so polite in his life before.

Lesley took hers and sat on the edge of the bed, crossing her legs. "Well, what an exhilarating day it has been?"

"Yes, you could say that." Joey couldn't help admiring her shapely legs.

"What a terrible thing though – that fire?"

"Yes, disastrous."

He was finding it extremely hard in the pursuing silence to avert his gaze from those legs.

"Do you like my room, Joey?" Her comment at least gave him something else to stare at, for he was beginning to feel that she might think him quite rude to be continually ogling her. On the other hand, she might be enjoying this amorous attention from him?

Joey finished drinking his coffee, placing the delicate cup and saucer on the table. "Yes, it's – it's very cosy," he offered his opinion. Not that he was anything of an expert regarding the interiors of ladies bedrooms, that is. Far from it, his actual knowledge along these lines being very limited indeed at this stage of his young life. But perhaps that was all about to change now that he had become better acquainted with Lesley?

"I'm very lucky to have such a nice place to myself right here in the heart of London. And both the Doctor and his wife are so good to me really."

"Are they?"

"I could definitely be working for a lot worse, that's for sure."

Joey leaned back on the sofa, crossed his legs, and began to feel more at home in his present surrounds. It was all a laugh really, him sitting up here in Lesley's bedroom in Harley Street sipping bloody coffee! He was certainly enjoying the experience though.

"What have you got planned for the rest of your week then, Joey?"

He gazed out of the window, noticing bright stars filling the dark expense above the rooftops of the buildings opposite.

"I'll probably go sightseeing – visit the museums maybe."

"The intellectual type, are we?" Lesley rose to her feet and placed her empty cup on the table in front of him.

Joey stood up also, sensing that perhaps it was time for him to leave. Not that he wanted to. In fact, he felt very tempted to reach out and take her hand.

It was Lesley though who moved closer to him, slipping her arms around his neck.

Here we go again, he thought with slight trepidation. But this time it felt different somehow, more natural.

Her blue eyes searched his. "Would you like to see me again sometime, Joey?"

"Yes, I would, Lesley, very much – tomorrow, if you like." He pulled her gently toward him and they found each other's lips as they kissed briefly.

"I'd like that too," she murmured softly.

They then kissed again, for much longer this time.

"I think you had better run along now, Joey." Lesley broke free from their fond embrace.

"Yes, I suppose I had better." He would do as she bade him, even though it was with some reluctance. "What time shall I see you, Lesley?"

"Any time after three."

"I'll phone you."

"Please."

She opened the door and walked with him to the top of the stairs. "Good night then, Joey."

"Good night, Lesley. Thanks for the coffee."

She pressed his hand. "You can let yourself out, can't you?"

He bounced jocundly down the stairs into the hallway below, opened the big, black wooden door and descended the marble steps into the street outside.

He crossed over the road, glancing back over his shoulder up at Lesley's room. It had been an extraordinary day.

Chapter 13 Sightseeing

He rose early the following day, Sunday. Outside, the sun shone brightly yet once again and the sounds of chirping birds in full chorus filled the quietness of this end-of-week morning.

After breakfasting, he went back up to his room to read more of the Hemingway novel. Eventually, he closed the book, went across to his drawer for some money. He took what he thought would be enough to cover his expenses for the day, put the remainder back. Not that there was all that much left. The fire had certainly made sure of that. He would probably have to cut short his stay in London now because of it.

Later on, after lunching at the restaurant in Baker Street, he crossed over the road and walked down the Underground to telephone Lesley.

"Doctor Duncan's residence..!" Lesley answered his call almost immediately.

"Hello!" The sound of hearing her voice again thrilled him immensely. "It's Joey."

"Oh, hello – how are you today?"

"I'm fine, thanks."

"Where are you calling from, Joey?"

"Baker Street Underground."

"I'll meet you there in five minutes if you like?"

"Yes, I do like."

"Don't go away now. . ?"

"No, I won't – I promise." He heard her laughing. "Bye for now then. . ."

Five minutes later, as promised, she came walking towards him dressed in a pretty blue summer frock that showed off her sunburnt arms, shoulders and neck. She was without makeup and wore open-ended sandals on her feet with her toes peeking through the ends of them. Her short, fair hair looked neat and tidy and shone in the sunlight. A small leather bag with long straps hung from her well-rounded shoulder. Joey felt excited just watching her.

"I hope I haven't kept you waiting long?" She greeted him with a smile, slipping her arm affectionately through his.

"No, you're very punctual indeed." He gazed into her beautiful eyes that were the same colour as the blue summer sky above them.

"I always try to be."

"Me, too."

"I trust that you will never keep me waiting?"

"No, never."

They stood looking at each other for a moment, a moment no doubt that they both wanted to remember and to be able to recall at some time or other in the future to remind them of their meeting together like this.

"Well, where are you taking me then, young man?" Lesley finally broke the moment between them.

"Do you like walking?"

"As a matter of fact, I do."

"Good – come along with me then."

"To the ends of the earth."

They both laughed as they crossed over the road at the traffic lights and proceeded to walk down Baker Street.

"Cricket flannels not in fashion today then, I see?" Lesley made light of his state of dress to that of yesterday.

"No – not today, luv."

As they strolled along they looked in the shop windows and at various buildings of interest to them, especially the British Telecom Tower that showed prominent over the tops of all the others way off to their left.

Lesley pointed to it. "Have you ever been to the top, Joey?"

"No – have you?"

"No – but I must someday."

"Perhaps we can go together?"

"That would be nice."

She squeezed his arm gently and smiled up at him as she rested her head momentarily on his shoulder.

They came down to Oxford Street, and then turned right to head in the direction of Marble Arch.

"Where are we going, may I ask, Joey?"

"I thought we might pop along to Speakers Corner for a while."

"Oh, I've never been there before."

"Haven't you?"

"I've never gotten round to it really."

Their walk quickened.

"I use to come here a great deal when I was at Lord's." Joey reminisced fondly.

"What actually happens there?"

"Oh, all kinds of people stand up to air their views and opinions on various topics – religion and politics mostly."

"I see. It sounds very interesting, I must say."

"It certainly can be, with heated arguments frequently breaking out between certain sections of the public. They're usually harmless enough though."

It took them almost ten minutes to cross the road to get in to Hyde Park. It would have been wiser to make use of the subway; but instead they weaved and bobbed their way between the cars and the buses and the motorcycles that raced toward them in a never-ending procession on their way down to Mayfair. When they had finally made it safely to the other side, they both laughed out loud at their utter foolishness.

"Proper madhouse, isn't it?" Joey's comment about summed up the exercise.

"I'll say it is." Lesley looked relieved to be standing on the traffic-free concourse by the entrance to the Park.

They came upon the scene before them with its green trees and green grass visibly picturesque in the back ground, whilst in the foreground crowds of people gathered together in groups on the expanse of tarmac to watch and listen to various individuals perched on wooden platforms delivering their speeches.

A loud, disapproving jeer went up to their left, this difference of opinion being directed at a dark-haired, dark-skinned man standing on his soapbox positioned beneath the branches of a huge chestnut tree, the leaves of which danced about in the calm breeze immediately above him. Brilliant sunshine filtered through the leaves, falling onto the side of his handsome face. He was dressed entirely in black. Shirt, black; leather jacket, black; black leather trousers; black leather boots. Perched askew on top of his head was a black leather cap, and covering his hands were even black leather gloves fastened together on his wrists by silver press-studs.

"This-a my friends. !" he spoke with an Italian accent, retaliating to the noisy crowd, pointing to a red flag he was holding aloft in his gloved right hand, his white teeth gleaming bright in the sunlight.

"You ain't-a gotta no friends. . !" a voice mimicked him from the crowd.

"I have-a friends, my-a friend." He smiled as he looked down at the congregation below him, his red flag fluttering in the breeze. "I have-a followers...followers of this-a red flag of freedom!"

He stood to attention suddenly, thrusting his gloved fist out in front of him, the smile disappearing from his face, his dark eyes gazing out over the heads of everyone. "Us-a fascists will-a win!" he spat out, gnashing his teeth.

The crowd howled with laughter at this statement and posture from the leather-clad Italian standing above them, both Lesley and Joey joining in with the hilarity.

"Win-a what, Charlie?" another heckler was quick to crack.

"Allow-a me to continue, lease!" The speaker pleaded patiently for silence from the overzealous crowd as he rested his arms on his soapbox.

"Get on wiv it then, for chrisake!" The intonation in the voice from the crowd made everyone perfectly aware that they had obviously lost theirs by this time.

The Italian then slowly removed the glove from his right hand to allow him to pull a clean, white handkerchief from his jacket pocket to wipe his perspiring brow with. After replacing it, he said very calmly: "Thank you. Now – where-a was I...?"

"With the bloody fascists!" The sound of another agitated voice echoed across the tarmac.

"Yes- a my friend. Mark-a my word – it will-a come to this-a country!"

"Rubbish!" An irate listener made known their feelings on the subject.

"It will my-a friend! Why do you not-a wish it...?"

"Free country – that's why! Don't want your sodding dictators here, do we?"

Choruses of: "That's right!" "Hear! Hear!" greeted the speaker.

The Italian waited patiently for the commotion to die down. Then, with added venom in his voice, hissed: "What the hella you already-a got in this -a country now then? You gotta Tory dictatorship! You gotta Socialist dictatorship! When willa you people wake up? When willa you learn?"

Jeers and boos greeted this part of his speech, someone shouting at him furiously: "We don't really wanna know mate!"

Joey felt Lesley tugging his sleeve as they stood at the rear of the gathering, more people arriving with regularity to witness the commotion that was going on all around the Italian orator.

"Doesn't everyone get upset so easily?" His companion seemed unable to take her eyes off the gentleman in question up on his soapbox.

"They most certainly do." Joey couldn't but help notice how many different nationalities of people there were milling about on the tarmac on this fine Sunday afternoon. "The one day in the week when everyone can speak their own minds if they wish, I suppose."

"It's all very interesting, I must say."

"Where else in the world would you be allowed such freedom of speech, I wonder?"

"Nowhere, really, I suppose." Lesley peered up at the agitated speaker as he held aloft in the air his red flag once again.

"I tella you truly." The rhetoric resumed from the man once more.

But cries of: "Go flag a bus down!" And: "Watch wot yer doin' wiv' that, mate!"

These comments from a couple of individuals in the crowd interrupted his speech.

"I tella you truly," the dark-faced man persisted, intent on being heard, "this-a very flag I'm-a holding will fly from the top of the White House in Washington before this-a year ees-a out!"

Uncontrollable laughter greeted this statement.

"How hilarious!" exclaimed Lesley, laughing out loud.

"Yeah, proper comedian, ain't he?" Joey commented, finding it all very amusing himself.

"You can-a laugh," the Italian continued, "but it willa be so. Then we-a fascists will have-a won!"

He stood to attention, threw his gloved right hand out in front of him again in a form of salute, head held high, a proud look on his stern face.

"Heil Hitler!" someone chanted.

The speaker lowered his flag, a smile now spreading across his smooth-skinned face. "My-a friends. . .!" he began again quietly, resting the flag at his side, unclipping a glove, pulling the white handkerchief from his pocket once more to dab his warm brow. "We willa win! Time alone willa tell! Then you willa see it is the truth I've-a been speaking."

"Why don't you go jump in the Serpentine!" an angry bystander suggested.

Events then got a little bit out of hand as people began shouting all manner of rude remarks at the speaker.

"Do you think we might find someone else to listen to, Joey?" Lesley requested nervously, obviously alarmed at the ferociousness of some of these comments.

They moved away, strolling along the tarmac, others doing likewise.

"He seems to be attracting a rather large audience?" Lesley pointed to a small, plump man dressed in a shabby looking brown religious habit, his fat fingered hands clasped together as he leaned forward on his soapbox to address the crowd.

"Yes, he most certainly does," Joey agreed, spotting the man in question. "We've heard enough politics for one day, I think – so let's listen to some religion instead, eh?"

"If we are to have ever lasting life..." They could hear the monk preaching as they drew near to him. "...Then we must turn to God and to our Savior the Lord Jesus Christ! Only then will we be saved – be purified of our past sins, and forgiven. He is there for all who seek Him. Believe me, you will never be sorry if you do. He will guide you and be with you always..."

"Is that a fact then?" a tall, unshaven, unkempt looking young man standing with hands in his pockets asked sneeringly.

"Yes, my son." The monk looked down at him.

"Then perhaps you'll ask Him to guide me. I've been bumming around and sleeping rough these past six months. See if – ask Him if there's anything going for me, will you?"

"Why don't you try asking Him yourself, my good friend?"

"I don't think I'm in favour with Him at the moment, Mister monk."

The monk unclasped his hands to let some rosary beads dangle between his fingers, a silver crucifix glinting in the sunlight, hanging from it. "That's where you are wrong." His soft, brown eyes were fixed on the young man below. "You are in favour with Him – more than you will ever know. He's waiting for you. Go to Him – at least try..."

The young man only shrugged his shoulders at this suggestion, thrusting his hands deeper inside his trouser pockets. "It's all a make-believe bloody dream, monk!" he growled indignantly.

"You think so, do you..?"

"I know so. Oh, you like to believe that there's something at the end of it all – this sodding awful life! But we all know there is nothing, absolutely nothing!"

"You are only speaking for yourself, young man."

"Am I?"

He turned to face the crowd, pulling a hand awkwardly out of his pocket. Then, raising his voice, asked: "Tell me, is there anyone here who doesn't agree with my point of view in this matter?"

The crowd remained silent.

He swung round. "There – you see, Mister monk!" he snarled at the religious man. "It's all a bloody lie! And you know it is."

The monk leaned forward, was about to make a reply, when the young man suddenly snatched the rosary beads from his hands and hurled them into the crowd. "Hypocrite!" he screamed at the top of his voice, turning on his heel, before losing himself within the thronging populace.

"I say! What terribly bad manners," a thin, bowler-hatted gent standing alongside Joey exclaimed in disbelief at witnessing such outrageous behavior from the young man.

"Here's your crucifix and beads, sir!" A middle-aged woman wearing a green headscarf confronted the speechless, red-faced monk as she handed them back to him after having recovered them.

Joey and Lesley spent the whole afternoon mingling with the crowd and listening with interest to various other individuals spouting off on one subject or another. They then noticed a little, white-haired old man carrying a sandwich-board that hung heavy-looking from his stooped shoulders strolling by in front of them with the words EAT AT ERNIE'S painted in large black letters on the front and back of it.

"Fancy eating there, Joey?"

"We'd probably never find the place," Joey replied with a smile.

His remark made Lesley laugh. "I'll go where thou leadest me then, young man."

"Fancy a cuppa, do you?"

"I do, rather, yes, Joey."

"Let's go then."

They found a snack bar close by. After securing a wooden tray each, they helped themselves to some sandwiches, cakes, and a pot of tea before paying a blonde-haired cashier for them at the end of the counter. They then went and sat at a vacant table over by the window.

"There we are, madam!" Joey arranged their things neatly in front of them.

Lesley unwrapped her cheese and tomato sandwich with a broad smile on her face. "Thank you very much, waiter!"

They sat in silence while they enjoyed their snack. Cigarettes followed.

"Thank you for a wonderful afternoon, Joey – I've really enjoyed myself."

"Good, I'm glad." He felt pleased with himself for having introduced Lesley to Speaker's Corner.

She looked at him for a moment. "You know, you are a very sweet boy."

Her remark made him blush somewhat. He had never been referred to as a sweet boy before. He quite liked it.

They continued talking together, informing each other of their likes, dislikes hopes and fears in life. They appeared to have a great deal in common. He had the distinct feeling that his relationship with Lesley would mean a great deal to him.

"Yes...I have a sister...she's married – lives in Birmingham..."

"Hasn't – didn't marriage ever appeal to you, Lesley?"

"I seriously thought about it a few years ago, yes. His name was Joseph. He was lead violinist with the London Philharmonic Orchestra; but then I discovered that he already had a wife."

"I see." He didn't really; but it sounded the right thing to say though out of politeness.

"You say you live with your mother when at home, Joey?"

"Yeah, still tied to her apron strings, I'm afraid."

She smiled sweetly at him. "What about your father?"

"He died just before I went into the RAF, unfortunately."

"Oh, I am sorry to hear that."

They smoked another cigarette and talked some more before deciding to leave.

Outside, the sun shone brightly, a perfect evening. They strolled along Oxford Street looking in shop windows, exchanging comments, smiling, enjoying each other's company. He really did feel at home with Lesley.

They turned into Langham Place, the British Broadcasting Corporation building situated to their right on the opposite side of the road.

"No doubt you know where this is, Joey?"

"The good old BBC – right?"

"Do you listen to the radio much yourself?"

"I'm fond of the music programmes and the Test Match cricket coverage, yes."

"We will have to go to a concert together sometime?"

"The Proms start this month at the Albert Hall, don't they?"

"Yes, I believe they do."

"I'll see if I can get some tickets for one."

She slipped her arm through his. "That would be nice," she said to him affectionately.

They walked on in silence, stopping finally outside a small public house not far from Harley Street.

"Fancy a drink, Lesley?"

"Thank you – I'd love one."

They entered the building. Numerous people were dotted about the bar drinking and talking. Purchasing some drinks from a tall, thin barman, they found themselves an empty table over in the far corner.

"We won't stay too long, Joey."

"Why, don't you like it here?"

"Very much – it's Monday tomorrow though and some of us have to work you know."

"Of course – I wasn't thinking."

She reached across for his hand. "I'd ask you up for a coffee, darling, but the Doctor and his wife will be returning soon from their week-end away."

"There's no need to explain – I understand," he said, a strange feeling coming over him with her hand in his, with her referring to him as darling.

She smiled. "Next week-end perhaps?"

"I'll take you up on that."

An hour and three drinks later they were still sitting at their table holding hands and talking incessantly.

"You say you are a Roman Catholic, Joey?"

"Yes, that's right."

"Me, also."

"Really?"

"Not a very good one I might add. How about you – are you still practicing?"

"Afraid not."

"We should be, you know."

"Should we?"

She looked at him quizzically.

"Do you not go to church at all now, Joey?"

"Very rarely," he confessed to her with honesty.

She caressed his hand affectionately. "Darling..." she sighed.

Joey moved forward in his chair to be closer to her.

"You're a very sweet boy?"

"Am I?"

"Yes, and I'm frightened I may lead you into something you might regret?"

"Why should I regret anything, Lesley?"

Her bright eyes searched his. "It's bound to happen between us, you know."

"Is it?"

"You won't think I'm...?"

"What?"

"Well, what I'm trying to say is that I hope you won't think any the less of me, will you?"

"Of course I won't."

She offered him a smile; but she looked sad. "You see – I couldn't bear it if you did. Tell me one thing, Joey?"

"Yes?"

"That when it's over you won't regret having met me?"

He looked at her thoughtfully for a few moments, feeling rather puzzled by her comment.

"Does – does our relationship have to end before it's even begun then?"

"No – but it probably will," Lesley informed him rather abruptly, removing her hand from his. "Look at it this way, Joey. You're on leave from the Air Force. We meet because of it. We find we care very much for each other. An affair follows, after which you return to your way of life, I, to mine. Please don't misunderstand me, Joey. I want it to happen very much with us, but I'm not fool enough to believe our relationship can last. After all, I'm a great deal older than you."

"And far more experienced at this sort of thing," he added sharply, and then wished he hadn't, biting hard on his lip.

"What exactly do you mean by that remark, may I ask?" Lesley questioned him coldly.

Joey wanted the ground to open up and swallow him. "Nothing – forget it."

"What kind of woman do you take me for?"

"I'm – I'm sorry, I shouldn't have said what I did."

Anger showed on her face. But then she suddenly smiled and took hold of his hand again. "Our first argument," she commented quietly.

"And entirely all my fault."

"No – I should have known better. Let's just forget it happened. Anyway – we better be going."

They finished their drinks and bade the barman farewell.

Outside, the sun had gone down the sky and a cool breeze was blowing. They walked in silence the short distance back to Lesley's apartment in Harley Street.

"Thank you for a wonderful day, Joey. Will you phone me tomorrow?"

"Yes, if you like."

Lesley slipped her arms around his neck, stood on tiptoe to kiss him. Then, breaking away, she pushed open her door and went in.

He came down the marble steps to strike joyfully out on the journey back to his hotel.

Chapter 14 Romance

The week that followed proved to be a very happy one indeed for Joey. He saw Lesley every night, and, together, they got on very well. He managed to get some tickets for one of the promenade concerts and they sat in the Albert Hall enjoying listening to some wonderful music. He had always been grateful to his teacher at his secondary-mod school for having introduced him to the world of classical music. He could remember even now being taken to his local Town Hall together with two or three other interested pupils by this man in his endeavour to convert them from pop to serious music. Where Joey was concerned he had certainly succeeded.

"Did you enjoy the concert, darling?" Lesley asked him afterwards over a drink in their usual pub.

"Yes, I did, very much," he answered, savouring a cool beer.

"It was a lovely evening, Joey."

"I'm glad you were there to share it with me, Lesley."

"Do you really mean that?"

"Of course I do."

"You are a very sweet boy."

"So you keep telling me."

"Well, it's true."

"Honest?"

"Honest."

They had another drink and sat holding each other's hand.

Then, from their tall barman friend came the cry: "Time, gentlemen, please!" Closing hour for the British pub!

They strolled back to Harley Street, a wonderful starry sky in the dark firmament above them.

"We get on very well together, don't we, Joey?"

"Like a house on fire, luv!"

"I-I'm glad we do." Her reply appeared to be somewhat hesitant.

"You don't sound too sure of this, Lesley?"

They came to a halt below the white, marble steps of the doctor's residence. "I think you know the reason for this." She looked deeply into his eyes.

"About hurting me, you mean?" He couldn't help but admire her beauty with the streetlights silhouetting her attractive face, her eyes sparkling.

"I am concerned for you, yes."

"I'm sure you have no need to be." He offered Lesley an assuring smile.

She began to climb the steps. "I have to go now, Joey."

"Shall I phone you again tomorrow?"

"Yes, please do. Good night then." She looked down and blew him a kiss.

Then she was gone, a feeling of sadness, loneliness creeping over him, only the twinkling stars above seeming to bear any relationship for him with life, with reality on this particular night in London town.

This feeling was to persist until meeting her again the following evening at the Coffee Shop in Baker Street.

"Have you had a nice day?" she enquired over the chatter from fellow diners.

"I spent most of the time thinking about us," he told her truthfully, noticing the pretty pink costume she was wearing, her general appearance pleasing him greatly.

"I trust they were all nice thoughts?"

"What else could they be?"

Lesley gazed at him inquisitively. "Did you come to any conclusions?"

"No – not really, other than that I'm pleased we are together, that's all."

"Are you?"

Joey heaved a deep sigh. "I just like the way things seem to happen naturally between us."

"You're very sweet, Joey."

After finishing their coffee they each smoked a cigarette.

"Right – let's go, shall we?" He had planned a surprise for Lesley that he hoped she would like.

She stubbed out her cigarette in the thick glass ashtray. "Where to, may I ask?"

"To the ends of the earth."

"Sounds great fun to me."

They left the Coffee Shop, turning down Baker Street in the direction of Regent's Park.

"Taking me to the Park, are you?" She sounded excited by the idea.

"Could be." He couldn't resist teasing her.

They crossed the Marylebone road at the traffic lights.

"It certainly is a nice evening for a walk," Lesley commented as they hurried along, the Park plainly visible a hundred yards or so away in front of them. "Assuming we are going for one, that is?"

"We're not really, no."

"Where are we going then?"

"To a Midsummer's Night Dream! that's where."

"What on earth..!"

"Want to come along?"

She gripped his hand tightly. "Don't tease, darling."

"I'm not," he lied, smiling with amusement.

"Yes you are. Now, where are you taking me?"

They entered the Park, flowerbeds on both sides of them ablaze with colour and sweet smelling to their senses.

"Ever heard of the Bard, Lesley?"

"The what..? Oh – Shakespeare, you mean. Well, of course I have, silly – who hasn't?"

"Well..?"

"Well..?"

They crossed over the wrought iron bridge that spanned the lake with its ducks swimming freely about in the water below them. Birds filled the air with continual song.

"Oh! Now I see," she exclaimed suddenly. "We're going to the Open Air Theatre, aren't we? What a marvellous idea."

"Do you think so?"

"Yes, truly wonderful."

"I wasn't at all sure you would like it."

She leant her head on his shoulder and sighed: "Of course, you do realize that this is somewhere else I've not visited before, don't you?"

"Really?"

"Really. You would think I would, wouldn't you? – living just round the corner from here as I do."

They made their way into the Park's Inner Circle, passing the restaurant, green lawns and flowerbeds to the right and where people were leisurely strolling about enjoying the tranquil scenery here on this pleasant summer evening. They followed the pathway that eventually led them to the Theatre. Here, they purchased tickets from a little, white-haired man who sat in an opening of a tall privet hedge that encircled the perimeter of the Theatre. Once inside, a young female attendant greeted them and then proceeded to show them to their seats, which were positioned about half way down from the front of the stage on the sloping grass verge. Most of the seats were now occupied and a continuous hum of conversation filled the calm night air.

"It's like being in another world, isn't it?" Lesley commented, gazing about her in wonderment.

With the setting sun slowly dropping behind the cast of players on stage, they both sat and enjoyed immensely the production of this renowned Shakespeare play. Joey admitted to himself that yes, it really was like being in another world as it brought back memories for him of afternoons spent in his old classroom studying the works of this great playwright, one in particular – The Tempest - coming to mind for some strange reason.

They applauded with the rest of the audience when it was all over the whole cast of the Play as they assembled on stage below them to take a well-deserved bow.

"I really did enjoy that, Joey." Lesley's reaction to the play was obviously one of sheer pleasure.

"Yeah, great wasn't it?" Joey couldn't help but agree. He also felt extremely pleased with himself for having thought of the idea of coming to the Open Air Theatre in the first place. After all, he didn't know if his companion was a lover of Shakespeare, did he? It could have been disastrous if she hadn't.

They strolled back through the Park, the evening quiet, peaceful, the calm lake free from boats at this time of day. They went and sat on a bench overlooking the water. They cuddled up close to each other and stole a kiss, not caring who saw them. Then they ambled back to Harley Street as dusk gradually descended.

"It has been a wonderful evening, Joey." Lesley smiled her appreciation for his benefit as they sat in their usual pub, the bar crowded, and a hum of conversation as ever present.

"Yes, it certainly has." He lit their cigarettes. "I've enjoyed it very much."

"What will I do for amusement when you go back to camp, I wonder?"

"I'm sure you'll find something of interest to occupy yourself with."

"You think so?"

They sipped their drinks.

"Will you phone me again tomorrow, Joey?"

"Of course I will," he assured her with a smile.

"Have you anything planned?"

"I'll think of something to surprise you."

"I love surprises."

"Yes, and you never fail to surprise me."

He ordered some more drinks for them from the barman, and, after returning to their table, quietly asked Lesley: "By the way – how is the Doctor and his wife these days?"

She leaned back in her chair and crossed her elegant looking legs. "Oh, they're fine – just fine."

They sat talking, drinking, smoking, totally engrossed in each other's company. Then they left to stroll arm in arm together slowly back to Harley Street. They kissed in the shadow of the doctor's doorway before saying good night to each other.

The following day he phoned Lesley and asked her to join him for lunch at a restaurant down in Baker Street, the sun shining gloriously yet once again outside in the crowded streets. They enjoyed a hurried lunch together before Lesley returned to the doctor's residence in Harley Street to resume her duties. They met again that evening for dinner in the West End, travelling there by taxi.

"You shouldn't go to all this expense on my part, Joey," Lesley commented as they sipped an excellent glass of white wine together.

"I wanted us to share a meal to remember like this before I return to camp," he insisted. "And anyway, I was hungry."

Lesley was right though. He would have to try and not be so extravagant with his money. He was fast running out of it.

The next morning he finished reading the Hemingway novel before going for a walk in Regent's Park. It was another glorious day as he strolled by the lake watching the ducks swimming in the water, people walking to and fro. He even spotted the tramp he'd seen on his first day absent in London. He was still rummaging through the litterbins along the water's edge, hoping to find something of use to him.

He crossed over the small bridge by the boat shed and stood with his arms resting on its wooden rail to look out across the lake.

"Mornin', sir!" A voice belonging to that of a weather-beaten face of a sailor-hatted old man sitting by the boat entrance, greeted him.

"Hello! guvner," he acknowledged the old fellow.

"Gran' day."

"It sure is."

"On holiday, are yer?"

"Sort of, yeah."

He shot Joey a look through bushy eyebrows. "Fancy takin' a boat out, do yer?"

Joey deliberated with his suggestion.

"Exercise'll do you good..?"

He walked slowly down through the open gate. "Yeah – why not?"

"That-a-lad."

The old fellow steadied a craft for him in the water by the mooring. "Take 'er beyond the bridge up there an' back." He placed a short-stemmed pipe in the corner of his mouth.

Joey climbed into the vessel and sat himself down on the broad, wooden seat, taking hold of the smooth-ended oars in the palms of his hands.

"Right, lad." The old boy pushed him out.

He moved slowly away down the centre of the lake with the warm sun above beating down on him. He suddenly began to feel wonderfully free, contented and happy with life at that precise moment in time. He wished the feeling could go on forever.

Out in the middle of the lake he shouldered both oars of his boat, beads of water hanging from them as he drifted idly along. It was calm and peaceful here with just the gentle sound of the water lapping against the sides of his boat. His thoughts turned to Lesley. He knew now that he was growing very fond of her, and it frightened him a little because he realized he was in no position to commit himself to her fully owing to his present circumstances. After all, he didn't really have much to offer the good lady now, did he? He had the feeling he was getting himself involved in something that was way out of his depth, and that if he wasn't careful he would almost surely drown when the truth concerning the deceitful life he had been forced to lead since going AWOL became known to her. Should he therefore tell Lesley the truth and risk damaging their relationship or should he just carry on as he was, living a lie until found out? His inexperience in matters such as these left him feeling unable to decide one way or the other. He supposed in the end though that he would just leave things as they were.

He stayed out on the lake for about a half an hour before returning to the boatshed. He had enjoyed his morning row very much indeed.

"Thanks, lad." The old man welcomed him back with a warm smile, securing the craft safely. "Enjoy yerself?"

"Yeah... I did," Joey panted from his rowing efforts.

"Cheerio to yer, then lad."

"So long, old fellow."

He decided to go for a coffee in the restaurant by the Theatre, crossing the iron bridge on his way, stopping for a while to look at the colourful illustrations of the Park's wild life on display inside the glass frames there. Reoccurring thoughts of Lesley however, kept troubling his mind. Was he perhaps falling in love with her? he contemplated. She was considerably older than he, which made him feel that this love – if indeed it were love – would ever last? And what were her exact feelings toward him? He couldn't quite believe that such a mature woman could conceivably be falling in love with him, a mere youngster half her age? As he had observed earlier, he had absolutely nothing to offer her. His so-called career in the RAF was over, ending in disgrace with him now in danger of becoming a deserter. He had no clear plans for his immediate future. No prospects either. Despite this rather gloomy outlook though, he felt good about things in general and decided to go where life was presently leading him and worry about its consequences later.

After drinking his coffee, he caught a bus down in Baker Street that took him along to Oxford Street where he decided to do some window-shopping to take his mind off things.

Everywhere was crowded and the traffic was extremely noisy and before he actually realized it he found himself standing in the middle of Piccadilly Circus with its people and its pigeons.

He entered a jeweller's shop close by. It would be nice to buy Lesley a present. After some considerable browsing, he decided to purchase a fine-linked gold chain and cross for her that he was sure she would like.

The rest of the morning he spent looking in more shops before relaxing on a bench by the water fountains in Trafalgar Square. He then treated himself to a ploughman's lunch in a pub across the way in the Haymarket, washing it down with a couple of cool beers. The bar was crowded with city gents doing likewise, conversation prominent.

Afterwards, he visited the National Gallery where he spent an hour or so admiring paintings, being particularly interested in the colourful landscapes by various artists on display.

He then journeyed back to Baker Street via the noisy Underground to his hotel where he had a nap before taking a refreshing shower, after which, a visit to Lord's Cricket Ground to watch the final hour's play between Middlesex and Warwickshire. He sat drinking a beer in front of the Tavern in the sunshine.

At close of play he found a telephone kiosk to call Lesley from.

"Have you had a nice day, Joey?" The sound of her voice made him realize how much he had missed her company.

"Pretty good – yeah," he replied to her question.

"You can tell me all about it when I see you."

"When will that be, Lesley?"

"Oh...in about five minutes. If you want me to, that is?"

"I'll be waiting outside the Planetarium for you."

"Sounds exciting?"

"You like the idea?"

"Yes, very much - although I have a confession to make to you, Joey."

"What's that, pray?"

"That I've never been to the Planetarium before either."

"Really? Well, I am surprised to hear that, Lesley."

"I'll see you shortly."

"All right."

He walked out of Lord's, jumped on a bus that took him down to Baker Street.

Lesley was waiting for him when he arrived. She looked as attractive as ever, dressed in blue slacks and a white, short-sleeved blouse.

"You're late?" she teased with a smile, taking hold of his hand.

"And you, as well as being very attractive, are very punctual," he told her truthfully.

"In which case I will forgive you, young man."

"You had better." It was his turn to tease now.

They stood looking at each other for a moment, people walking past them and in through the glass-door entrance to the Planetarium for the start of the show.

They eventually did likewise and began climbing the stairs that led them into the dome shaped building after having paid their admission. They were shown to their seats, which were about half way down on the side they came in, the theatre beginning to fill quickly.

"I never imagined it would look like this from the outside," Lesley commented, gazing about her. "You've been here before, have you, Joey?"

"Yes, I have."

"You seem to have visited most places of interest in London, don't you?"

"No, not really, just a few."

The theatre lights dimmed, and, up above, the dark dome suddenly became alive with thousands of twinkling stars. A bearded gentleman then began speaking into a microphone on a platform below them, a complicated, telescopic instrument positioned to the left of him.

"Welcome to the London Planetarium, ladies and gentlemen!" his clear, distinct voice echoed through the loudspeakers. "My name is Professor Watkins and I am going to be your guide on this journey to the stars."

Joey felt Lesley's warm hand in his as they gazed up at the starry sky, various well known London landmarks silhouetted against the skyline of the dome.

The complete show lasted about an hour, during which time the professor explained in detail the various aspects of the galaxy and its wonders. It left them with their minds boggling, to say the least. Then they rose from their seats to troop off out the building with the rest of the audience, who, no doubt, were in the same state of complete overwhelmingness after this exhilarating experience.

"Enjoy the show, did you, Lesley?" They were now back outside in the street, the evening pleasant, the sun drifting down the sky, a cool breeze blowing.

"Very much indeed." Lesley was acclimatizing her eyes to the sudden brightness after the contrasting darkness of the theatre.

"Fancy a drink?"

"I'd love one, Joey."

They strolled along to their favourite pub.

Joey got them some drinks from their friendly barman and then joined Lesley at their usual table over in the corner, the bar quite crowded.

He lit their cigarettes.

"Anything exciting happen for you today, Joey?"

"I've been having a great time," he informed her, blowing smoke across the hazy barroom. "I actually went for a row in a boat out on the lake in Regent's Park this morning."

"The energetic type, eh?"

"I also took a stroll round the West End before having a pub lunch. Then in the afternoon I paid the National Gallery a visit. Finished my day off by popping up to Lord's to watch some cricket this evening."

Lesley sipped her iced gin and tonic. "You certainly did have a nice day then. Too busy, I suppose, to spare much thought to yours truly here then?"

"That's where you are wrong, Lesley."

"Prove it," she teased.

He produced his present for her out of his pocket, placing it on the table. "There – is that proof enough for you?"

She looked at him for a moment. "Darling!" she uttered finally in amazement. "I didn't mean...honestly..."

"Just a little something I picked up for you today whilst shopping. I hope you will like it?"

She slowly opened the lid of the small box in front of her, gazed inside, and took out the gold cross and chain. "Oh, Joey – it's beautiful! How charming, but you shouldn't have."

"Nonsense!"

She reached across for his hand. "You really are a very sweet boy," she said to him softly.

They enjoyed several more drinks before the evening ended, Lesley slipping her unexpected gift carefully around her shapely neck and smiling happily.

"It has been a truly wonderful evening, Joey." They were standing on the steps outside the doctor's residence back in Harley Street once again. "Thank you for your lovely present. I will treasure it always."

They stood together holding hands and gazing into each other's eyes, not wanting the evening to end.

"I'd invite you up, Joey, but I'm not sure what the Doctor's reaction might be." She slipped her arms around his neck and kissed him. "They do say patience is a virtue though."

"W-what do you mean?"

"Well, the Doctor and his wife will be going away this week-end, so..." she whispered seductively in his ear.

"Will they?"

"So, the house is going to be empty, isn't it, silly? We can drink an awful lot of coffee during that time, can't we, darling? Good night then, Joey." She pulled him closer, finding his lips with hers again.

"Good night, Lesley," he said to her after a long, lingering kiss together.

Then she was gone, disappearing behind the large door, leaving him to wander slowly back to his hotel.

The following day, Friday, it rained. Not heavy, but enough to make him stay in bed for best part of the morning. Hunger, however finally drove him down to Baker Street for something to eat and where he also phoned Lesley from to make arrangements to meet her in the Coffee Shop nearby.

"What a miserable day it is," Lesley commented whilst folding her umbrella after having vigorously shaken the raindrops from it outside in the street before sitting down next to him in the cafeteria. "So – what have you been up to then?"

"Apart from lying in bed all morning – not much really."

"You lazy old thing you."

They smoked a cigarette each.

"Got anything planned for this evening, Joey?"

"I thought we might pay The Wizard of Oz a visit."

"The what?"

"The Wizard of Oz!"

She looked at him quizzically for a moment before smiling the most beautiful smile as the meaning of his words dawned on her. "Oh! the cinema, you mean?"

"Yes, it's showing next door. Fancy going?"

"I'd love to, yes. Judy Garland, isn't it?"

"That's the one."

They left the Coffee Bar and walked the short distance to the cinema, light rain still falling from an overcast sky. Joey got their tickets at the foyer and they found some seats in the back row before settling down to watch the film.

During the interval they munched popcorn together. They then both enjoyed this classic film very much indeed, becoming totally engrossed in the magic of its characters and outstanding musical score. At the finish they stood for the national anthem and stole a kiss in the dark before the lights went up.

They hurried round to their favourite pub for a couple of drinks just as last orders were being called.

"I'll phone you again tomorrow, Lesley," he told her, stubbing his cigarette out in the ashtray on the table.

"No, not tomorrow, Joey." Lesley's serious tone of voice reply startled him somewhat.

"Why – have I done something wrong?"

She squeezed his hand gently. "No, of course you haven't, silly. I just want you to call round at Harley Street for me instead at about four-o-clock, all right?"

"Yes, all right, if you wish." He felt somewhat perplexed by her request.

"It's – it's just that I have a surprise waiting for you, Joey."

They walked back to Harley Street in the rain before bidding each other farewell and parting company.

Joey hurried along to his hotel wondering to himself what on earth Lesley had planned for the following evening.

Chapter 15 Caught In The Act

The next morning he ate a hearty breakfast. No one else was using the dining room, not even the old couple, he noticed. Perhaps they had left? Outside, the weather appeared to be back to normal with the sun shining gloriously yet once again. He drank a further cup of tea before going on up to his room, passing the manager on the way standing behind his desk and looking as efficient as ever.

"I trust you are enjoying your stay here with us, Mr. Webster?" he enquired politely.

"Yes, very much so, thank you." Little did the guy know he couldn't possibly afford to remain longer. His present financial circumstances wouldn't allow it. "Could I settle my account up with you when I go out, please?"

"Are you leaving us then, sir?"

"Yes; unfortunately something has come up."

Up in his room Joey counted what little money he had left. A fear of running out proved to be true, and there was no way he could prolong his visit. By the time he paid cigar-smoking Sam his dues downstairs he'd be lucky to have enough to keep him in food for another week. Perhaps another night here, two at most, was all he might manage. He would settle with the manager now though, then see how things worked out for him. He began cursing that fire at the Cricket Club for getting him into this mess. Especially as he and Lesley were now growing extremely fond of each other.

He suddenly spotted Tony's cricket flannels hanging over one of the chairs. He should return them to him really; but he didn't fancy the idea of going back to Southbank again. Last week was great fun, sure; but to return there now would only make him feel even more inferior than he did before. Different class of bloody people, Joey boy!

He stuffed the cricket trousers into a carrier bag to take down to Harley Street. Perhaps the doctor could return them for him sometime?

He settled with the hotel manager, and then went for a walk in the Park to think things through. After all, he'd have to find somewhere to stay if he wanted to continue with his adventure. Reporting back to camp didn't appeal to him as an option just yet, that's for sure.

He spent the morning strolling round enjoying the sunshine. Then he went for a bite to eat down in Baker Street, after which, a journey along to Lord's yet once again to watch the cricket for a couple of hours. A bus ride then back down to Baker Street on his way to visit Lesley, the time on the clock of Abbey House, three-forty-five.

He arrived at the doctor's house and pushed the doorbell.

"Is that you, Joey?" Lesley's voice echoed from a metal speaker attached to the wall close to his ear.

"Y-yes..." he stammered, startled somewhat by the unexpectedness of her suddenly greeting him in this way.

"Do come on up, darling!"

The door opened automatically and he hurriedly stepped into the hallway.

"Hello!" Lesley's friendly voice and presence greeted him from the top of the stairway.

He began climbing the stairs, running his hand along the polished banister rail, Lesley gazing down at him from above, smiling. He went up to her and she slipped her arms around his neck and kissed him tenderly.

"How are you, Joey?" her soft voice purred in his ear.

"Fine – I'm fine." He felt a little nervous though as he allowed her to take his hand and lead him into her room where they sat down on a sofa, a small table in front of them set for tea.

"You have timed your entrance just right, Joey."

"Yes, so I see."

"My little surprise for you – I hope you like it?"

Their eyes met and Joey began to feel excited.

"You make a start while I pour the tea."

He tentatively helped himself to a small, pyramid-cut shaped sandwich.

"Here you are, darling! Please help yourself to sugar."

They sat in silence while they slowly sipped their tea. Lesley then asked him what he had in the bag.

"Cricket flannels!" he explained. "Tony's – remember? Do you think the Doctor could return them to him for me sometime?"

"Yes, I'm sure he wouldn't mind, Joey."

They finished drinking their tea and sat smoking a cigarette, the bright sunlight outside streaming in on them through the open window.

"Right! we'll go then, shall we?" Lesley's suggestion came as a complete surprise to him.

"What do you mean – go? Where to..?"

"For a taxi ride to begin with."

"A taxi ride?"

She smiled. "Yes, one's due here any minute."

"Is it really?"

He felt somewhat disappointed, being under the firm illusion that he and Lesley were going to spend some time alone together here in Harley Street.

"I have a further surprise in store for you, darling!"

She got to her feet, looked down at him with her hands outstretched and helped him slowly to his feet. "Don't look so sad, Joey. We'll only be gone a couple of hours."

"Will we?"

"Yes, I promise."

She embraced him lovingly, and Joey began to respond by pulling her warm body closer to him; but she pushed him away gently, saying: "No not now, Joey - later."

The taxi horn honked in the street below.

"That's our transport." Lesley moved toward the door, scooping up her handbag from off the chair on the way.

They hurried downstairs to the waiting cab that immediately whisked them away on their journey to the GPO Tower after Lesley had informed the driver of their destination.

"Now this is one place that I've not been to Lesley," Joey confessed to her after she had paid for this unexpected treat for them and they had entered the building after alighting from the taxi.

A tall, uniformed man stood before them inside the open doors of a spacious lift that eventually took them to the very top of the Tower. They crowded inside with other members of the public, the doors closing quietly behind them. Then they were propelled upwards, the lift seeming to increase in speed as it rose swiftly towards its destination, the complete journey lasting only a few seconds before it finally pulled to a halt at the top of the Tower. The doors slid open and they stepped out onto a circular, glass-partitioned Viewing Tower that looked out over London.

Lesley led him over to one of the large windows. He began to feel insecure at such a precarious height, but after some reassurance from his charming guide, he very soon got used to these conditions.

"Look!" she said excitedly, slipping her arm round his waist. "Isn't that a wonderful sight to behold?"

Joey gazed out at the beautiful scene before them and for a moment was at a loss for words.

"It-it's fantastic!" he stammered finally.

Lesley pointed downwards. "See! There's the street we came along in the taxi just now."

He peered below, rooftops of houses and numerous office blocks slowly becoming plainly visible. He even spotted people and cars, so small from this height, yet easily recognisable.

"And there's Harley Street!"

Yes, Joey could even see that also.

"And Lord's Cricket Ground! Over there! See, darling?"

He looked. "Yeah, I can see it." Who'd of thought it? Not much of the old place. Just a glimpse of the white wooden-rail boundary fence and the green grass beyond it.

"There's Regent's Park!" Lesley resumed with her sightseeing commentary. "Spot the lake?"

He looked, he saw, he marvelled at it all. Yes, there was his beloved Park and the lake with the bright sunlight glistening on it.

They moved slowly round the Viewing Tower, other people gazing out at the various landmarks of London. They spotted the Houses of Parliament, Big Ben, the Tower of London. And there was London Bridge with the river Thames, some small tugboats even visible on the glassy water as they steamed away from them. There was St. Paul's Cathedral, Trafalgar Square, The Mall, Piccadilly Circus, and Buckingham Palace. In fact, the whole of London, even further out on this clear and sunny evening.

Then it was suddenly all over for them as they journeyed back down in the lift to find themselves safely on the ground outside in the street where they walked slowly arm in arm back to their little pub.

"Did you like my surprise, darling?" Lesley asked him quietly when they were sitting in the pub at their usual table enjoying a drink.

"Marvellous! It really was," Joey thanked her jubilantly. "I never knew London could look so beautiful."

She took his hand and gazed intently into his eyes. "You do realize I'm growing very fond of you, don't you, Joey?"

His eyes avoided hers for a moment, her statement making him feel just a little embarrassed.

"Are you?" he finally said to her awkwardly.

"You must know that I am," she sighed, squeezing his hand.

He gazed into her blue eyes. "I-I like you a lot as well, Lesley," he confessed to her bravely, but not really feeling completely at ease in a situation of this nature somehow.

She leaned forward closer to him. "Do you, Joey?"

He held her gaze. God! She had beautiful eyes. "Yes, and I'm glad we met that day at Lord's, Lesley."

"You're so sweet, my darling."

He finished his drink. "Shall we have another?"

"All right – just one more before we go, eh?"

Twenty minutes later they returned to Harley Street, the evening cool, pleasant. Up in Lesley's room he sat on the sofa while she cleared away the tea things. Joey felt nervous and couldn't quite believe that they were about to make love together.

After tidying up she came and sat down next to him. "You look wonderfully handsome, young man," she complimented him, taking his hand, her delicate fingers entwined in his, sending shivers down his spine.

They sat in silence, while outside a cool breeze came in through the open window. Down in the street below it was very quiet. Only the chirping of birds could be heard.

"Would you like to take a shower, Joey," Lesley suggested, smiling beautifully. "Freshen up – you know?"

"Yeah – all right," he agreed, rising, looking down at her, excited by her attractiveness.

He returned fifteen minutes later feeling fresh and relaxed. Dusk had descended outside and Lesley had the lamp lit by her dressing table. He noticed an uncorked bottle of wine on the coffee table with two long-stemmed glasses by its side. He sat down on the sofa next to her.

"Feel better?" she enquired.

"Much – thank you."

"Help yourself to a cigarette while I pour the wine."

He lit them both one while she filled the glasses.

"There we are, Joey."

He raised his glass, she doing likewise.

"Here's to us then, darling!"

"To us, Lesley."

"May we always be happy."

"Always."

They touched glasses before sipping the wine.

"Delicious!"

"Very nice indeed," he agreed.

They sampled more, their eyes searching each other's, the room darkening with evening drawing to its close.

Suddenly, Lesley jumped to her feet and cried out excitedly: "The proms!"

Surprised by her enthusiastic outburst, Joey asked: "What about them?"

"They're on," she said, hurrying over to her table to turn on the radio. "It will be nice listening to them over our wine, darling!"

"Yes, I suppose it will," he agreed, stretching his legs out in front of him.

She rejoined him as sounds of an orchestra filled the room. Both of them remained silent for quite some time as they listened to the last movement of a melodious Brahms symphony, at the end of which Lesley asked if she could get him a bite to eat.

"No thank you, Lesley." Food was the last thing on his mind at that present moment as he sat there feeling relaxed and very peaceful.

"I can easily get you something – no trouble," she whispered, turning to face him, her arms suddenly encircling him, pulling him close to her.

His heart began pounding wildly, shattering his brief spell of repose.

"Joey, darling..."

"Yes..." he whimpered weakly, finding her warm, inviting lips with his. He could hear further music in the background being played again. Then they were suddenly rolling around on the floor together, fondling, caressing, and kissing one another passionately.

"Let's go to bed," Lesley panted in his ear.

They picked themselves up from the floor, still locked in an embrace.

"You get undressed," Lesley whispered as she clung close to him, "while I pop along to the bathroom for a moment."

With difficulty, they finally broke away from each other's arms.

"Pull the curtains across, Joey."

He did as she requested, then, after Lesley had left the room, slipped out of his clothes and slid his naked body down between the cool sheets of the bed to wait patiently for her to join him, his heart beating wildly inside him, his mind full of thoughts of what it was really going to be like with her, knowing now that everything was all right and that nothing could possibly go wrong at this stage of the proceedings.

She came through the door again and he watched her walk across the room dressed only in a flimsy white negligee, her beautiful curved body on view for him to look at and admire.

"I hope I haven't kept you waiting too long, darling," she spoke to him softly before stepping out of her night attire, wearing nothing now but his gold chain and cross and looking breathtakingly lovely.

His heart went out to her.

She reached for his hand after drawing back the sheets, and he slid over toward the wall to let her climb in the bed beside him.

"Darling!" she uttered, her arms enfolding him, their bodies suddenly becoming one, and with the oneness, the slow, rhythmic movement of their love-making together with gasps of joy coming from both of them until finally and in unison they clung close in consummating their act of love for each other.

They then lay side by side listening to the music from the radio that quietly filled the room as they both drifted off into a relaxed state of slumber.

Then, quite suddenly and without warning he felt himself being shaken vigorously.

Opening his eyes, he saw Lesley standing over him and heard her exclaiming in a restrained, horrified voice, "Wake up! Joey – the Doctor's outside!"

He lay on his side, her efforts to awaken him not really having much effect on him at that precise moment, his mind being in a state of semi-consciousness.

"Please!" her hysterical voice bade him again. "He's in his car down in the street outside!"

This final statement from Lesley immediately seized him with terror, bringing him quickly to his senses, making him sit bolt upright in the bed.

"What!" he hissed frantically.

"The Doctor's here! He'll be on his way up in a minute!"

He jumped out of the bed and hurriedly dressed himself. "W-what shall we do?"

"God knows!"

He stood petrified in the middle of the room trying desperately to think of a solution to their dilemma. "Where will the Doctor head for, Lesley?"

"His room, I suppose."

"Where's that?"

"Right next door to this one."

"Oh, my God!"

Joey heard the front door open and close. Footsteps sounded in the hallway below, then on the stairs. He saw Lesley's frightened looking eyes glued to his as they heard a door in the room next to them open and then the sound of a light being switched on and of curtains being drawn.

"Do you think he will hear me if I sneak down and let myself out?" he whispered.

She grasped him by the hand. "I-I don't know."

"What if he catches me?"

"I could lose my job, I suppose."

"We certainly don't want that."

They stood together in the middle of the room not knowing what to do for the best. A thought then suddenly occurred to Joey.

"Is there a drainpipe outside this window, Lesley?"

"I-I'm not sure." Her whispered reply sounded frantic.

"Turn off your light, would you?"

She did so, throwing the room into an eerie darkness.

"What are you going to do, Joey?"

He drew the curtains across quietly, light from the street lamps outside entering the room. "I'm not sure yet," he whispered, carefully opening the tall window and stepping out onto the small balcony in the quiet stillness of the early morning.

"Please do be careful!"

He noticed a drainpipe within easy reach on the wall to the right of the balcony. It travelled all the way down to the basement below. Coming back in to the room and taking Lesley by the hand, he whispered to her confidently: "I think I can manage. There is a drainpipe outside."

"W-what if you fall?" He felt Lesley's hand tremble in his.

"I'm more worried that someone might see me."

"That's hardly likely at this hour of the morning."

"What is the time then?"

She glanced at the illumined hands of her small clock on the dressing table. "It's just after three-thirty."

"What on earth's he bloody well doing coming home this time of the morning?"

"I don't know – I honestly don't know."

Joey turned his shirt collar up. "Well – here goes then!"

She kissed him quickly on the cheek. "Do be careful, darling! Give me a call Monday, won't you? Not tomorrow – just in case the Doctor suspects something."

As he stepped back out onto the balcony he began to feel like the guy in the Cadbury's advert on tele, 'And all because the lady loves Milk Tray.' Secretly though, this turn of events made him feel quite excited. Who would have guessed it would end in this way? he thought. All that it needed now was for the police to catch him shinning down this bloody drainpipe at this hour of the morning and he'd really be for the high jump. Especially here in the middle of bloody Harley Street of all places.

On his slow descent down the pipe he looked up at the dark abyss above him and at the many stars dotted about in the heavens and at the full, bright-shining moon hanging there motionless.

Arriving safely on the ground below, he ran quickly up the basement steps onto the pavement, and then hurried across the road. He glanced up to see Lesley waving to him before drawing her curtains.

He walked briskly along Harley Street not knowing whether to go to his hotel or not. He decided he wouldn't, fearing that patrolling policemen might spot him and question what he was up to in the streets of London at this unearthly hour. Instead, he found himself wandering in the direction of Regent's Park with the idea of maybe hiding there until sunrise?

He found the Park gates locked when he got there. Suddenly, car headlights appeared out of nowhere in the darkness, startling him as they picked out his solitary figure, throwing his shadow twenty yards or so down the pathway in front of the hedge that ran round the Park.

He heard a deep authoritative voice ask: "Where do you think you're goin', lad?"

Joey peered through the window of the car and noticed two uniformed policemen looking out at him.

"Trying to find somewhere to sleep," he told the officers sheepishly.

"Where have you been then?"

He thought for a moment before offering them an explanation.

"West End! Missed me last train home," he said finally.

Eyes scrutinised him menacingly from inside the panda car.

The driver laughed. "And the best of British, mate!"

"There's a gap in the hedge further down," his colleague kindly intimated before their vehicle moved off down the road and disappeared in the darkness.

Heaving a sigh of relief at their departure, Joey went to investigate. He soon found the opening and stepped through into the safety of the Park, moving quickly and silently across the grass to where a large tree with overhanging branches was situated close to the lake, the water sparkling in the bright moonlight. He located two deckchairs that were stacked in a pile on the grass nearby. After erecting them, he sat down on one, put his feet up on the other and folded his arms across his chest. He would endeavour to get some sleep before dawn's early light.

Chapter 16 Humiliation

He remembered awakening on a number of occasions in his effort to sleep, to keep warm. And keeping warm proved the most difficult. He finally managed though to drop off for an hour's slumber before being alarmingly brought back to life by a wet tongue licking his face and a man's voice commanding: "Down, boy! Down!"

With his head bent low on one side, Joey quickly opened his eyes, only to see others, those of a huge Alsatian, in fact, staring at him with a long, red tongue hanging from its open panting mouth. And towering above him stood a rosy-faced, heavily built, six-foot tall park keeper.

Joey sat up slowly from his hunched position on his deckchair-bed. "Mornin'!" he greeted his early morning callers. The sun had risen in a clear blue sky that was visible through the leaves and branches of the tree directly above him.

"And good morning to you!" the man addressed him gruffly, intimating to Joey that he was about to be seriously reprimanded by him. "Don't you know that it's against the law to sleep here in the Park?"

"I-I'm sorry, but I missed my last train home last night... The police told me it would be all right to kip here. I had nowhere else to go, did I?"

The uniformed man pulled at the dog's lead and sloped off, the animal busy sniffing the ground on route.

"You're all right this time, lad - but don't make a habit of it, that's all!" the park keeper called to him over his shoulder.

"No, I won't," Joey assured him, although there was no guarantee he wouldn't now that his finances had all but dwindled. One more night's stay at the hotel, and that was it really.

He looked out across the lake. The remains of a mist hovered above the surface of the water, a sure sign that it was going to be another warm day.

He rose from his makeshift bed and slowly began making his way out of the Park, his body achingly stiff after his spell in the deckchair. However, the nice weather and the sounds of birds in full dawn chorus very soon helped him to forget these aches and pains.

He came down to Baker Street, the roads free from traffic on this bright Sunday morning in London town. He noticed a group of pigeons hopping about on the pavement outside the Milk Bar by the Underground Station busily pecking at the remains of an abandoned bread roll. They rose noisily in the air as he approached, their wings flapping vigorously. He crossed over the deserted road, his stiffness now having disappeared.

Five minutes later he slipped unnoticed through the lobby of his hotel. He took a hot bath, shaved, looked closely at himself in the mirror, half expecting to see a change in his appearance because of his experience with Lesley last night; but he detected none. Reflecting upon the episode, it seemed such a damned shame that the Doctor had ruined it all for them. It was all so humiliating.

He went straight to bed, dropping off into a deep sleep, a sleep he did not come out of until later that evening.

Chapter 17 Reflections

After enjoying his final breakfast in the hotel the following morning, Joey sat looking out of the window, the streets outside noisy with traffic again as another busy Monday morning came to life in the heart of London.

It was a woman, middle-aged, dark-haired with full red lips that settled his bill when he finally left the hotel.

"I hope you enjoyed your stay with us, Mr. Webster?" She offered him a warm, farewell smile.

"Very much." He felt sad at the thought of now actually having to leave.

"Goodbye then, sir! Do come again."

He slung his holdall over his shoulder. "Yeah, I might just do that." Somehow though he felt that this would be highly unlikely. He'd always remember it with affection though.

Outside, he heaved a deep sigh and strode off in the direction of Baker Street again. Crowds were now prominent everywhere and there seemed a sense of urgency about the way everyone hurried to and fro in the bright sunshine. A swarm of people suddenly emerged out of the Underground as he crossed the road by the traffic lights. He stopped to watch this mass of life as it then dispersed to head off in all directions. He felt somewhat out of place. Where the hell did he fit into everything? he wondered to himself. They all seemed to have a sense of direction, a purpose in what they were doing, where as he seemed lost in comparison. He began to doubt whether or not he would ever fit in with the rest of society?

A bowler-hatted gent carrying a briefcase swept by. Shapely, attractively clad ladies bore down on him to accompany him across the road as he found himself getting caught up with them, then with shop windows, huge office blocks, chattering people, noisy traffic, all making their presence felt, until finally he found himself standing in Oxford

Street. And there he stopped, wanting to be rid of them all. Noticing a book shop close by, he ducked quickly inside. Even at this hour of the morning a few avid readers were browsing among the bookshelves. Joey decided to join them.

Two hours passed by before he was to eventually emerge from the shop, having leafed through a few books that had caught his attention. It was while he was doing this that he became aware of the untold amount of literature there was waiting to be discovered. He suddenly wanted to become part of this world. For the time being though it would have to wait.

His thoughts turned to Lesley. He needed to talk with her, so he slipped quickly down into the Marble Arch Underground to locate a telephone kiosk to call her from.

"Doctor Duncan's practice!"

"H-hello! May I speak to Miss Williams, please?"

"Who is this calling, please?"

"Mr. Webster!"

"Is that you, Joey? How the blazes are you, ol' boy?"

"I-I'm fine, thank you." Fears that the doctor may have detected his presence in Lesley's bedroom the other night appeared to have been unfounded judging by the man's genuine friendliness towards him now on the phone. He felt pleased, for it meant that Lesley's job was safe after all.

"I must say that innings of yours the other Saturday was a superb one, ol' chap. Ab..so..lutely superb. When are you jolly-well going to play for us again?"

"When you've jolly-well built a new pavilion!" Joey laughed jokingly.

"We'll have one completed and ready for the start of next season. Until then we're having to make do with ol' Dick Benton's stable to change in..." A slight pause, then "... I'm afraid Miss Williams isn't here at the moment, Joey."

"Isn't she?"

"No – her sister's been taken very ill in Birmingham apparently."

Joey could hear a train down below in the Underground screeching to a halt.

"I'm sorry..." the doctor's voice continued, "...is there anything I can do?"

"N-no, thanks," Joey stuttered before hanging up the phone.

He climbed slowly and dejectedly back up the stairs out into the sunlit, crowded street once more, and crossed over the road to the Corner House for a coffee. He felt quite saddened to learn that Lesley had left town.

After a drink and a cigarette he walked blindly down Oxford Street again, feeling somewhat lost and very much alone. For the first time during his stay in London he realized he was without any set plan for the day. Lesley's departure had certainly thrown him. There was also the question of where he would stay at night now that he had finally checked out of his hotel?

As he wandered aimlessly along, an idea suddenly came to him.

"Of course!" he said out loud, stopping dead in his tracks. "The Southbank Cricket Club!"

He could find shelter there somewhere – a haystack or something in Dick Benton's field? Yes, he was beginning to feel happier already.

Regent's Park loomed in front of him and he immediately felt himself being drawn toward it.

Once inside, he revisited the Open Air Theatre in Queen Mary's Gardens once more. He managed to squeeze through an opening in the hedge and stood for a moment looking down at the deserted stage below him. Then, walking between the vacant wooden seats, he stepped up onto the boards of the Shakespearean platform. He didn't really know why he was doing this. He just felt a sudden compulsion to somehow. Advancing toward a balcony used by members of the cast, he climbed to the top of it to gaze out at the empty rows of seats before him, at the trees on the green, grassy banks, at the hedge running along the top of the Theatre, his hands resting on the balcony's iron rail. A line from one of the Bard of Avon's works that he vaguely remembered from schooldays came to mind, summing up his feelings and why he happened to be there in the Theatre. He couldn't remember exactly how it went, but attempted it nevertheless.

"All the world's a stage!" he spoke out loud. "And the people in it merely actors! Each has a part to play...!"

He paused for a moment, his hands still grasping the balcony rail, the famous words he had just uttered clear in his mind.

"Yeah – we are merely actors!" he repeated to himself excitedly. "And we all do have a part to play!"

He turned, came back down the stairs. Then, standing at front of stage with legs astride, arms folded, he said in a clear unfaltering voice: "But surely it's how we play the part we are given that really matters in the end!"

With these, his own words, ringing in his ears, he began making his way out of the Theatre and back down toward the lake and beyond to Baker Street. From there, he caught a train to Harrow-On-The-Hill, his destination, the Southbank Cricket Club.

He walked the short distance from the station up to the cricket ground. Stepping onto the green turf of the sports field once again, he immediately noticed the absence of the Club's pavilion, recalling vividly the memory of it burning down that night he was last here. He stood where it once used to be, a blackened concrete base all that was left of it now. He viewed the picturesque little ground before him. A great deal had happened since his arrival here a week ago; and he had been a part of it all, had experienced everything, had found himself involved in another world that he never knew existed.

He spotted the Club's old green-painted roller standing idle to the right of the Tea Hut. Without fully realizing what he was doing, he found himself turning the handle of the door to this building. It opened, and he stepped inside. A metal sink unit ran along the wall below the window, and he noticed an electric power point on the wall close to the door with a red light glowing where someone had forgotten to switch it off. He turned the hot tap on. Boiling water poured out. Joey knew then that he would make this his hotel room for the remainder of his stay in London. A large wicker-chair stood in the corner, while on a hook behind the door hung a couple of white umpire coats. His bed and blankets! All this, and hot and cold running water. What more could he wish for?

Joey spent the remaining hours before darkness sitting beneath a tree over in a corner of Richard Benton's field watching the setting sun slowly disappearing down the sky like a huge shining copper penny.

Chapter 18 Military Escort

For the remainder of the week Joey travelled to and fro from Harrow to London, returning late of an evening to sleep in the Southbank Cricket Club's Tea Hut. He spent his days watching the cricket at Lord's, and phoned Harley Street regularly every morning to enquire about Lesley; but there was still no news of her.

And so his final week in London came to an end. He felt bitterly disappointed at not seeing Lesley again; but somehow he knew he wouldn't. He would remember her always though with strong affection.

On the Sunday evening he decided to pay his mother a visit to spend his last few hours of freedom with at their home before returning to camp the following morning to face the music.

It was after midnight when he let himself in the small house he had been brought up in, this humble abode surrounded by others of similar design in a poor area of town. He chuckled quietly to himself as he thought about the very select company he had been keeping lately and of their wealthy houses. He was convinced now more than ever that there was indeed another world outside the very limited one he had been led to believe only existed and was determined more than ever also to find that world, to become a part of it. He would first of all though have to get this unfinished business with the RAF sorted out.

He spent the night downstairs sleeping on the sofa, his mother being in bed when he arrived. He found the sofa to be much more comfortable than the wicker-chair ever was.

The following morning he was awakened by his mother with a most welcome hot cup of tea, something that of late he had certainly not been accustomed to.

"I managed to get a week-end pass, Ma," he began explaining his presence to her, sipping the hot drink.

His mother eyed him with suspicion. "Did ye now?" she questioned him in her beautiful Irish brogue.

Joey hated having to lie to her; but what else was he supposed to say? If she only knew, he thought, gazing up at her, at her wrinkled brow and grey hair. Did she perhaps dream of another world, another life for herself other than this humble one? he wondered.

"Then perhaps ye'd be good enough to tell me why the poleece are waiting outside the house, Joey?"

"The what?" he shrieked with alarm.

"It's true enough me boyo – they're wantin' to accompany ye to the station, they tell me."

What on earth could he say? He'd been found out.

"What have ye been up to, Joey?"

Whilst getting dressed he explained to her what indeed he had been up to these last weeks. Her only reply to this knowledge was: "Ye certainly seem to have been doin' some gallivantin' about, that's for sure!"

He bade his mother a fond farewell, telling her not to worry and that things would be all right. He felt sorry though that his visit had been cut so short in this rather undignified manner for him.

"Don't go upsetting yourself now, Ma. I'll let you know how things go just as soon as I can."

The police patrol car stood menacingly in the road outside their house, no doubt giving the neighbours something to brighten up their day.

He got in the back of the vehicle and sat silently between two uniformed officers as they pulled away on their journey down to the police station. It saddened him to have it all end in this fashion, especially where his mother was concerned. He would have much preferred going back to camp under his own steam. Not this way – made to feel like a bloody criminal.

At the station he was bundled out of the car and led inside where a rather overweight sergeant ordered him to empty his pockets. His few belongings, along with his holdall, were then transferred to a locker for safekeeping. He was left feeling somewhat bemused by it all and couldn't quite believe what was happening to him.

"Wait over there until you are called for, son!" the sergeant then ordered him, pointing to a chair by the wall.

He appeared in court at ten-o-clock. Standing in the dock, he was then confronted by a red-nosed official perched in his seat of office high above him. None other than the Judge himself! There were other numerous people gathered in the courtroom; but he paid them no heed.

"Corporal Webster!" the Judge addressed him sharply.

Joey stood to attention in the dock, his hands down at his sides in military fashion.

"No, sir!" he corrected the old geezer's mistake. " It's Airman Webster since losing me stripes."

Dressed in faded robes of office, the old boy fumbled with some papers on his desk in front of him.

"Yes – well – be that as it may..."

"I thought you should know, sir! Just to put the records straight, sir!"

The Judge glared angrily at Joey, obviously annoyed at this oversight.

"Airman Webster!" he continued emphatically. "You are accused of being absent without official leave from the Royal Air Force since the thirtieth of July. Do you plead guilty or not guilty to this charge?"

"Guilty, sir!" Joey had no other option other than to admit this. It would be no good denying it.

"You will be held in custody to await military escort!" He fumbled annoyingly with his papers once again. Then: "Next case, please! " The Judge dismissed Joey in a manner that suggested he had far more important business to attend to now that he had been referred back to the Air Force to be dealt with. Out of the court's jurisdiction, so to speak.

Much to his surprise, Joey then found himself being led down into the depths of the courthouse, descending steep concrete steps to the prison cells below where he was promptly locked up in one. Left on his own, he lay on the hard bunk bed to contemplate, his thoughts turning immediately to Lesley and of all they had experienced together since their meeting that day at Lord's. It seemed he was now paying the price for this. Not that he particularly minded as he actually felt a better person because of it. It meant having to accept his punishment like a man that was all.

A few hours later two RAF military personnel took him from his cell back up to the police station again. After being allowed to collect his belongings, he was then officially handed over into their custody.

"He's all yours!" the desk sergeant informed them upon release of his prisoner.

"Let's go then, Webster!" one of the military, a hard-faced looking nark, barked at him.

Joey swung his holdall up onto his shoulder, took a deep breath, and, flanked either side by his escorts, marched out of the building with them.

At the foot of the station steps he was bundled into the back of a service truck, the tailboard of which was then swung up and securely fastened on him and his accompanying escort before pulling out onto the road that would lead them back to camp.

He sat looking out over the tailboard at the roadway speeding along beneath him, becoming aware of the busy traffic passing to and fro, of pedestrians walking the pavements, of the blue expanse of sky above. And through this awareness, a realisation of how much existing life there was all around him. Life to be lived, to be experienced by all, himself included. There suddenly seemed so much to be done, to be tackled, with so very little time to do it in. He felt he couldn't wait to be part of it all.

A strong desire to jump out the back of the truck seized him; but he somehow managed to control this feeling. He would need to be patient and learn to wait until this present business had sorted itself out before returning to a normal civilised life again.

Twenty minutes later the truck swung in through the open camp gates and came to a halt on the tarmac outside the Guard Room. The tailboard was lowered and Joey stepped down with his escort. He spotted sergeant Cummins along with the sergeant of police hurrying towards him.

"You got the bastard then?" Cummins addressed the driver excitedly.

"Yeah – they got me," Joey got in quickly, looking his old enemy straight in the eye.

"What the hell do you think you've been up to, Webster?" Cummins confronted him eyeball to eyeball.

Joey stood upright, the bright sun above shining down on them. "Thought I'd enjoy a spot of leave, Sarge!"

The sergeant looked long and hard at Joey, unable to control his mounting anger.

"Is that a fact?" he snarled in Joey's face. "Well – we'll see what sort of bloody 'oliday we can arrange for you inside the Guard Room then, shall we, my son?"

Joey never flinched, never so much as looked at him. What could he do to him anyway? What could any of them do?

"Right, then, Webster!" the sergeant of police bellowed in his ear. "Let's be 'avin' you inside, lad! 'Eft turn! Qui...ck march!"

Flanked either side by his escorts, Joey turned smartly and marched briskly along to the Guard Room.

THE END

Don't miss out!

Visit the website below and you can sign up to receive emails whenever John Costello publishes a new book. There's no charge and no obligation.

https://books2read.com/r/B-A-YWQC-LPLO

BOOKS 2 READ

Connecting independent readers to independent writers.

About the Author

John Costello was born in Watford, Hertfordshire to Irish parents. As a young man he was engaged on the M.C.C. Young Professional Cricketer's staff at Lord's Cricket Ground and represented them in several matches at the famous Mecca of cricket prior to entering the RAF to complete his National Service. On returning to civvy street, he worked at numerous jobs: cricket coach, groundsman, insurance salesman, before retiring. It was then that he began writing as a hobby and went on to self publish some novels and short stories, mostly dealing with the theme of cricket. Recently though, he has written a novel about life in general, drawing upon his interests in drama and music which will soon be made available, besides other titles. At present his true story PHONE CALL TO SINATRA will also be made availabe soon. He now lives on the Isle of Wight.

About the Publisher

www.ingramcontent.com/pod-product-compliance
Lightning Source LLC
Chambersburg PA
CBHW050949120626
46552CB00001B/451